ARANSAS MORNING

ARANSAS MORNING

A NOVEL BY
JEFF HAMPTON

Jeff Hampton, Writer / JL Books and Creations
901 W. Avenue E
Garland, Texas 75040
www.jeffhamptonwriter.com

Publisher's Note: This is a work of fiction. Names, characters, places, and incidents are a product of the author's imagination. Locales and public names are sometimes used for atmospheric purposes. Any resemblance to actual people, living or dead, or to businesses, companies, events, institutions, or locales is completely coincidental.

Book Layout © 2014 BookDesignTemplates.com

Aransas Morning / Jeff Hampton -- 1st edition
ISBN 978-0-9966448-2-2

Cover Photo: Sunrise at Port Aransas, Texas, January 21, 2013. By Jeff Hampton.

Dedicated to the real Sam, whoever and wherever he may be, and to all the Sams out there who are searching for family and the true way home.

Acknowledgments

Writing a book is a journey, and there are many people who travel with a writer as he makes the trip. For me, those people have been:

- LeAnn, Melba, and Mom, who read my original short story and insisted there was a longer story that needed telling.
- Gary, Chip, Nancy, Tom—my writers group—who read each chapter with me as the story flowed out of my imagination, and whose encouragement, critique, and camaraderie ultimately propelled me from Chapter 1 to "The End."
- Gail, Steve, Jayne, Larry, and Michael, who gamely read my complete rough draft and gave me the gift of their honest opinions.
- Alison, whose eyes and instincts I would trust with anything I write.
- The good people of Port Aransas, Rockport, and Victoria, who provided the inspiration for the settings and characters in this story.
- And LeAnn, who read every chapter as it was written and pushed me to keep going, and who has been the steady center of my own story.

—Jeff Hampton

Chapter 1

Sam stumbled out of the trailer into the heavy predawn air. The only sounds that penetrated his otherwise empty head were a car speeding down the highway toward Corpus Christi and a couple of gulls fighting over whatever gulls fight over at six in the morning. With a big gap-jawed yawn, he started the short walk to the beach, the pavement rough and hard against his feet until he reached the place where the Gulf breeze blows sand onto the roadway. There, his arched soles relaxed into the powdery sand that was still warm from the late July heat.

A dozen yards farther, the morning quiet gave way to the eternal rhythm of the surf. Sam glanced left and right and was relieved to see few people out this morning. He yielded the beach to tourists from mid-morning until late evening, but he claimed the sunrise and sunset for himself. Except for a lone jogger, a couple sitting in plastic chairs and a few strollers, the coast was clear.

It was a world away from the crowded streets of Oak Cliff, across the Trinity River from downtown Dallas. A year earlier he'd headed south on the interstate to Waco, where, tired of the traffic, he dropped down through the belly of Texas on Highway 77. Cameron, LaGrange, Halletsville—all the way to McFadden, where the name Rockport on a green sign got his attention and he veered eastward toward the coast. He drove as far as he could, and when he ran out of road, he let the ferry take him the rest of the way.

Crossing the beachfront road imprinted with tire tracks, Sam picked his way across the hard-packed band of beach strewn with broken shells and seaweed and then onto the damp sand firm enough that you could write a name with your toes.

From across Port Aransas at the northern tip of Mustang Island, Sam heard the horns of the ferries crossing the channel with their morning cargo. He remembered the queasiness in his stomach that morning he first arrived as the solid ground suddenly became buoyant. He'd had the feeling once before—as a kid on a summer horseback trip when his mount dashed into the river and the bone-jarring trot gave way to the smooth synchronized pulse of four legs pulling through the water. It was exhilarating and frightening, and both times he wondered how the machine beneath him could stay afloat.

Sam crossed the channel just that once and traded his car for the lease on the rusty trailer in the little park between the condos and gift shops. It wasn't much, but a roof over his head and the sand beneath his feet was all he wanted. Eventually he scavenged a bicycle, but there was no longer any rush to get anywhere.

Sam waded calf-deep into the brown slurry and closed his eyes. Years ago, on a business trip to Florida, he walked on a bright white beach and cursed aloud when a wave flooded his tasseled loafers. He always regretted not pulling off his shoes and socks, rolling up his pant legs and letting his tired feet and weary spirit take a swim. Perhaps he would have gone back into the meeting more civil, more compassionate. Instead, he badgered a weak man into giving away all he had—losing a part of himself in the process.

A gust of wind off the Gulf blew Sam's fading yellow locks around the top of his skull and rustled the gray hair on his bare chest. He'd been on the island long enough to earn the leathery hide of a native beachcomber while his heart grew soft inside. "Live and let live" had taken the place of "winner take all."

As Sam walked and his eyes sharpened, a dark rock became a greasy oil filter and a glint of light revealed a tangle of gold and purple Mardi Gras beads carried down the coast from Galveston after Ike.

Sam had never weathered a hurricane but he knew the pain and destruction of living on the edge. He'd been a high roller in a high-stakes business until one night when the celebration got out of hand and he wrecked his car. Word got around town and none of his sales spin could stop the crash that followed. He lost his job, his home, his marriage. The people he mistook for friends turned their backs. He retreated to an apartment to plan a comeback that never materialized. Then came that day when he realized it was over and he packed the car.

Nowadays, the only "comeback" Sam had was to return to whatever job he was holding if it fit the wanderings of his spirit. Once a creator of trendy restaurant fads, he was content now to clean tables and sweep floors in exchange for meals and a minimum wage. Now, "branching out" meant leaving a restaurant gig to work on a shrimp trawler and from there joining a beach cleanup crew and then retiring to press slogans on T-shirts.

Sam came upon a long ridge of sand built up into a castle wall with finely carved battlements that had somehow survived the overnight tide. Back in his glory days he made an offer on a turreted mansion, but there was always someone with more money and better credit. He dreamed of being a king but he'd always just been a jester.

As the rising sun highlighted the clouds and foaming breakers with pink and orange, Sam came upon a man staring out across the water. Circling slowly, he saw the man's face painted with sadness yet anticipation. Sam edged up and leaned into the man's peripheral vision.

"Uh . . . hello . . . I was wondering . . . when you look out at the water, what do you see?" he asked.

"The love of God."

Sam nodded and started to walk away, but the man continued: "My wife . . . she died a year ago this morning. I drove all night to be here."

Sam stood still, letting the words drift past his brain and settle on his heart. "I lost my girl too," he said softly. "I lost everything."

Sam turned to walk away when the man spoke again.

"Wait . . . uh . . . excuse me, do you know if there's a coffee shop open anywhere this time of morning?"

Sam stopped a moment to think. "Just Shelly's."

"What's that?"

"Shelly's Dream Bean. It's back through town. I don't know the address."

"Tell you what, maybe you could show me and I'll buy you a cup of coffee."

Sam looked down at his bare feet. "I don't know, I'm not really . . ."

"Come on, this is Port Aransas, nobody dresses up here. I'm not too dressed up myself," he said, pointing to his shorts, flip flops, and wrinkled T-shirt. "We can sit outside if you like, or I'll bring you back here. Let's go," he said, motioning for his new acquaintance to follow him.

Silently they walked off the beach and back to the blacktop. Sam didn't risk a glance as their path brought them alongside the trailer park.

"I'm right here," said the stranger, pointing to the modest but clean hotel next to the highway. Digging into his pocket he pulled out his car keys and pressed the button. Thirty yards ahead of them a car chirped and the headlights flashed. Regretting his decision to come, Sam followed from a distance and hesitated at the back of the car as the stranger opened the driver's side door and said, "It's open."

Sam slowly opened the passenger door and paused to brush the sand off his feet and legs before getting in. When the door was shut, the stranger put the car into reverse and began backing out of the parking space. Turning sideways to check his blind spot, his glance caught Sam's and he stopped.

"I'm Dave," he said, and stuck out a hand.

"Sam," came the reply as he hesitated and then accepted the gesture.

"Good to know you, Sam."

With Sam mostly gesturing and saying "turn here" at the appropriate moments, they drove the short distance back into the heart of the town that was beginning to come to life with the rising sun.

"Can't get a good start without a cup of coffee," Dave said as they got out of the car and walked up the wood steps leading to Shelly's Dream Bean. A wad of bells jangled as he pulled open the door.

"What'll you have?" Dave asked Sam as he stepped up to the counter. Sam was standing back out of view and when he answered, "black coffee," the young woman behind the counter leaned out toward him.

"Well hey there, Sam, how are you this morning?"

"Fine," he said quietly and turned to stare out the window.

"That'll be two black coffees," said Dave, glancing from the girl to Sam and back again.

A minute later they had their coffee, and, after looking around the room, Dave motioned that they go outside. Sitting at a metal table on the plank porch that looked out toward a pier with a line of boats and the channel beyond, they watched the sun continue its rise, glinting off the masts and rigging that swayed in the morning breeze.

"So, you know the girl behind the counter?" Dave asked.

"Yes."

"You come here often?"

"No."

"But enough to know her?"

"We worked together for a while out on the highway."

"Oh really, where was that?"

"A restaurant, the Crab Cake."

"You waited tables together?"

"She waited tables. I cleaned up."

There was silence again and Sam hoped the conversation was over, but Dave had more questions.

"So now she's working here?"

"She owns the place. She's Shelly."

"Oh really. Well, good for her."

The conversation waned and Dave sensed it was time to take Sam back to where he found him.

"Well . . . ," he said, standing up and fumbling in his pocket for his keys. Sam understood the cue and stood up too. They rode in silence back to the hotel.

"It was good to meet you, Sam. I don't know when I'll be back down here, but when I am I might look for you on the beach."

Sam said nothing, so Dave stuck out his hand again and Sam shook it, lifted his cup a little in his left hand and said, "Thanks."

Sam started walking back toward the beach while Dave walked in the opposite direction to the hotel. Reaching for the side door, Dave looked back over his shoulder just in time to see Sam divert off the blacktop, turn into the trailer park and disappear inside the wood fence.

Chapter 2

Lying on his back on the small, lumpy bed, Sam cursed himself for being so foolish. He'd put himself in an awkward position because he stopped to ask a stranger a stupid question. He'd been on the beach for a year, and he'd never spoken to a soul, except maybe if someone asked directions. He'd surely never been the one doing the asking, and he promised himself he'd never do it again because look what it got him: a ride up the highway with a man he didn't know to get a cup of coffee he didn't need from a girl he didn't want to see.

"The love of God." Sam let Dave's words roll around in his head for a moment. He'd said it so easily—too easily.

"My ass," Sam said aloud. "What love? What God?"

Sam had grown up in the church. He knew the basics of faith, he knew the signature stories, including the one about Job who was beaten down by God but who kept on trusting and believing anyway. What kind of love was that, and what kind of faith did it take to love a God who would drive you into the ground?

"Insanity," he said. "That's what it takes."

He reasoned that this man Dave's veneer of serenity was coming out of a grief that was still fresh. Even a year out, grief has a way of holding you close to what you once had as if the act of grieving will bring someone back. But Sam knew differently. In time grief is replaced by loneliness and that leads to anger and doubt. And then . . . nothing at all.

Sam rolled over on his side. Through the cheap curtains on the little window he could see that the sun was rising high toward the noonday sky. By now the tourists had taken the beach, so Sam closed his eyes and drifted away.

Back in town, Shelly stacked coffee mugs next to the carafes. She'd had a good morning rush and now she took advantage of the mid-day slump to restock and replenish. The morning had started in its usual way with Bo coming in off his boat to fill his metal travel mug and pay for it with a handful of spare change and a mouthful of aggravation.

"Hope you've made it strong. You know I can't stand that weak stuff you push off on the tourists," he blustered. "I won't be having none of that."

Shelly looked blankly at him as he clanked the mug onto the counter.

"And better give me one of those cookies too," he said. "Don't have time for nothing else this morning." And then, under his breath, "Besides, you don't have nothing else worth having."

"You're lucky I let you come in here at all," Shelly replied. "If there was anyone else here right now I'd have to serve you in back by the dumpster where the other varmints feed."

"Naw, you'd be too afraid to leave the counter unattended," Bo volleyed. "Hey, when are you gonna let a man come in here and get this place going the way it oughta go?"

Shelly didn't answer. She'd known Bo long enough to know when it didn't do any good to answer back. She also knew that while he harbored some old-school chauvinism that came with his age, there was a touch of fatherly affection in his words, so she cut him some slack.

Bo's early visit kicked off the daily parade of shopkeepers, bankers, real estate brokers, and tourists. And in the middle of it all was the unexpected visit by Sam and the stranger. It was curious just in the fact that Sam had come in at all. Shelly hadn't seen him in about four months, certainly not since early spring; she remembered because it was still cool outside and Sam was wearing his tattered blue windbreaker. She had seen him at the market and told him to come visit her at the Dream Bean when she got it opened, and she opened it on the second day of April. What he had been doing since that time she didn't know, but evidently he had found a way to get by because he didn't look destitute. He looked like Sam had always looked: windblown, tired, withdrawn.

But then he had this unfamiliar young man with him, or was it the other way around? She couldn't tell for sure. The stranger was buying, and the two sat outside together and seemed to be talking about something. And they came and went in the stranger's car. They were clearly there together, but that's all she could deduce. She wasn't really worried about it, but it was all very curious just the same.

And then for a moment she allowed herself to think about the young man aside from his being with Sam. He seemed kind and amiable, perhaps too much to be running with a sad sack like Sam, which added to the curiosity of them being together. And as she went through their visit again she thought that perhaps the young man wasn't as young as he had seemed. Certainly he was younger than Sam, by a good ten years at least, but he wasn't a fresh-faced college grad like the ones that pestered her during spring break. In his early thirties, perhaps. Maybe late thirties. Forty, tops, and that would put him in her league . . . but then she shut down that thought because she knew it was a dead end. She knew nothing about this man, young or not, and she might never see him again, and on top of that she had a business to run and there wasn't time for any of that.

The rattle of the bells on the door shook Shelly loose from her daydreams. She slid her slim figure back around the counter and wiped her hands on a rag before looking up to greet the next customer.

Chapter 3

Dave always traveled light—something that he and Debby often bickered about—and it didn't take him ten minutes to pack his duffle bag, scan the room for any missed belongings, and slam the door shut. Walking down the long balcony to the stairs he could see down the road and out onto the Gulf of Mexico. He wished he could stay longer but he'd accomplished his goal—to remember Debby and spend some time alone with his memories.

As he walked, his eyes looked back up the road and fixed for a moment on the trailer park where he had watched Sam enter earlier that morning. Debby used to look across a crowd of people and say, "See all these people? We'll never see any of them again." He wondered if that would be true with Sam.

Dave got all the way to the Dallas County line when he realized that he had mindlessly rushed home. How many times had he promised Debby that they were going to slow down and make a day of it, stopping to look at things along the way? But they never did and he hadn't this time either; it finally sunk in that he was a destination man and not a journey man. With that conclusion drawn, he vowed not to bother himself about it again.

Pulling up to the house in East Dallas, Dave pushed the button on the remote and watched as the garage door slowly opened. In the year since Debby died, he had sold her car and he was now used to seeing the empty garage. Still, a part of him longed to see the car sitting there so that he could allow himself the brief fantasy of going in and finding her walking from the back room to ask, "How was your trip?"

That fantasy was long gone now and when he walked through the back door into the house he was met by the silence that had become familiar and expected. In that silence, Dave clung tightly to his habits, and that included unpacking quickly—getting the dirty clothes into the washer, putting his toiletries away, emptying his pockets. The latter action rendered candy wrappers, some folded tissues, and a receipt from the coffee run with Sam to the Dream Bean. Following another habit, he tossed the receipt into a desk drawer to be sorted out at tax time.

Two days later, Dave was back at his job but his enthusiasm was absent. If the trip south had done anything at all it had instilled in him the idea that he no longer wanted to waste his time working at something that did not interest or touch him. One of the few benefits—no, the only benefit, and it wasn't so much a benefit as an opportunity—that had come from his life as a widower was that he could make decisions that impacted nobody but himself. What's more, with a modest check from Debby's life insurance policy, he could afford to focus on things that he wanted to do and not just what he needed to do.

Among those things, he entertained the notion of spending more time in Port Aransas. Neither he nor Debby were from there, but Debby was from Victoria, eighty miles north. She had spent her childhood going to the beach and that had rubbed off on him. Before Debby died, he gently suggested that they could sell everything and spend her last months on the beach, but she said she wanted to stay home in Dallas, and so they did.

Now, as a single man, Dave considered the entire world as a potential destination. The Rocky Mountains, Europe, California, a coast somewhere. And now that he'd been back to Port Aransas, he was intrigued. He was much too practical to become a beach bum, as Sam apparently had done, but perhaps he could go down for a week or two at a time.

But not yet. His intuition—and his accountant—told him that he needed to wait a while longer before making big decisions. He'd been given that advice soon after Debby's death, and he'd followed it to the letter. He banked the life insurance money, went back to work, and generally resumed the life that he had, with only one difference: he was alone.

But it was a big difference—huge in fact. It changed everything. Nothing else that was normal in his life was actually normal at all. He discovered that even when he hadn't been with Debby, his heart and mind were with her. If something happened interesting at work, his subconscious would file it away as something to share with her when he got home. Every decision he made was through the prism of the impact it had on them as a couple. He didn't know where his life ended and hers started. Without her, he was incomplete. He was missing an arm, a leg. He could hardly function, at least not in a meaningful way. He went through the motions. From the outside, it looked like he was in full swing. He made deadlines and kept appointments. He spent time with family and friends. He smiled at all the right times and laughed at all the funny jokes. But inside, he felt empty and bleak.

The trip to Port Aransas was an attempt at closure. Along with marking the moment of Debby's death at sunrise, Dave made a move to embrace his singlehood. Just before Sam had stepped alongside him on the beach that morning, Dave quietly pulled the wedding band off his finger. For a moment he considered throwing it into the surf, but he couldn't stand the thought of someone with a metal detector finding it some day and hawking it for cash. So he tucked it into his pocket. When he got back to Dallas, he put it in a little box alongside Debby's ring and pushed it deep into a dresser drawer.

Nobody said anything about his newly naked finger except for Jeff, an old friend and colleague, who met Dave on the front walk at Chubby's Diner and noticed the change immediately.

"Aha. It's about time."

"Time for what?" Dave asked as he self-consciously shoved his hands into his pockets.

"Time for you to get back in the game. So, tell me, did you do it on your own, or did some little beach hottie talk the ring right off your finger?"

"That's just rude," Dave said.

Jeff was often over the top with his comments, but his heart was bigger than his mouth and he could tell he'd gone too far. He wrapped a big arm around Dave's shoulder and lowered his voice. "Sorry, man, I just mean that you've suffered a lot, and it's good to see you starting to look ahead. You're overdue for some happiness. Anyway, let's go inside, I'm buying."

Chapter 4

Behind his fluttering eyelids, Sam drifted back through time, years and years, past his unraveling to a day that was fresh and new.

He and Brenda had just married and moved into the little apartment at Lee Park. In his mind, he could see everything about that home they'd made together: the antique bed angled in the corner of the cozy bedroom; the five square windows that looked down through the trees to the street three floors below; the tiny den where they first lined up lawn chairs until they had enough money to buy a sofa.

It was a place of love and laughter. Yet, Sam was a little uneasy in those first days because his career had hit an early snag. They married after Brenda finished two years of graduate school while he honed his skills at the small college town newspaper. With her freshly inked diploma and his two years of experience, they both interviewed at the Dallas News. She landed a job right away with her extra degree, but he was just another young white male newspaper reporter—one of hundreds coming out of journalism schools. Nothing was offered and he had to look elsewhere, eventually getting his foot in the door at a small ad agency.

It was the booming 1980s and there was plenty to do for anyone willing to work hard and stay late. Sam distinguished himself quickly as a copywriter, and even he was surprised that he not only had a knack for it but enjoyed it. The words "sell out" that gnawed at him for several months eventually faded from his mind and a year after he joined the agency he was named creative director for a full account.

The promotion came after a meeting late one night when he and a junior partner got into an argument over a campaign for a new neighborhood restaurant concept.

"Look, Sam, I just don't think this is going to fly. The client is too conservative for what you are proposing."

"Good grief, Richard, more than 90 percent of these guys go out of business within six months anyway. Let's at least put something out there that the public will remember. The way you're going at it, you'll be calling them 'Just Another Burger Joint.' We've got to make some kind of splash if anyone is going to care at all—even for six months."

"Well that's easy for you to say because it's not your money you're spending."

"No, it's not my money. It's their money, but I'm betting they want us to do more than just sit on it and take the safe route. This is their chance—probably their only chance—to make a go of it. They're already risking everything they have. I don't think 'safe' is what they want."

Just then one of the senior partners stepped into the room, having overheard the argument.

"Sam, why don't you call them tomorrow and let's get them in here to make a decision. Get with the art department and work up some mock-ups of your two best ideas. We'll let them decide." And then without saying anything else—and without even acknowledging Richard—he was gone.

Within a week the clients were on board with Sam's concept and six months later patrons were lined up at two outlets with more planned.

From then on Sam could call his own shots and he soon had a half-dozen people under his direct leadership. A year later, he was managing multiple campaigns.

Brenda, meanwhile, was locked into a steady job as an assistant business editor at the paper—a position that paid well but still had her working afternoons and nights. With energy to burn, Sam stayed up late to wait for her and then, more often than not, they'd go out for a late dinner when she got home, sometimes at one of the restaurants that Sam was representing. One night during one of those late-night dinners, Sam was jabbering away about his hectic day when Brenda, trying to decompress, pulled his hand down from the wild gesture he was making and gently said, "Enough . . . enough."

~ ~ ~ ~ ~

A gust of wind hit the trailer hard and shook Sam loose from his dream. He looked around, confused at first, and then sat up on the edge of the bed and rubbed his eyes. Looking out the window, he saw the old blue Ford LTD next door that meant Bob was home from his job at the freight company. Sam didn't need a clock to tell him that he had slept the afternoon away. Earlier in his life he'd have wasted another hour or so obsessing about the lost time and opportunities, but today it just meant that the beach would soon be clear and he'd have it all to himself.

Sam stumbled across the floor, unlatched the door, and stepped outside just in time to be hit full in the face by a cloud of loose sand. Shaking his head and sputtering to clear his mouth, he set out down the road to the beach.

As he walked, the sound of the waves pushing shoreward echoed a part of the dream that lingered in Sam's mind—"enough . . . enough."

Chapter 5

The bells on the door jangled loudly as Bo burst through and crashed his way to the counter for his early cup of coffee. Bo's boat was docked just down the pier, and the proximity had quickly made him Shelly's most regular customer. That's not to say that he was her favorite customer; Bo had a bluster and bravado that didn't necessarily go well with her early-morning mood.

Although Shelly and Bo were both island natives, their paths had never crossed until she opened the Dream Bean. She knew just about everyone in Port Aransas, and if she didn't know them then she knew of them. She knew Bo in that way; she'd heard stories about the blustery captain of the *Cassie* who didn't know where he ended and everyone else began. If he wasn't stumbling over people, he was sure enough crowding them. But, he'd been a regular since day one and so she put up with his constant questioning and unsolicited advice.

Like during the week before she opened the shop. She was painting a seascape mural on a wall one morning when he walked right in and started in on her.

"Who are you?"

"Shelly."

"What're you doing here?"

"Getting ready to open a coffee shop."

"Coffee shop? Who needs a coffee shop? Folks drink coffee at home."

"Not all do."

"Sensible folks do."

"Have you had coffee yet this morning?"

"No, but . . ."

"See there, you'll probably be my best customer."

"Not likely. So who you running the place for?"

"For me."

"No, I mean who owns it?"

"I do."

"In your dreams, maybe."

"No, in my reality."

"You do? How'd that happen?"

"Easy enough. I bought it and now I own it. And if you'll leave me alone and let me get back to work I might be ready to open on Monday."

Bo just stood there a moment and then turned and walked out.

Shelly knew some real characters on the island, and Bo led that parade. Still, his regularity was enough to get her out of bed and get down to the piers to open the doors. She knew that if she was late he'd make a big deal out of it.

So, on this particular September morning, like almost every other one since she had opened, Shelly let Bo blow through the door and have his say.

"Hey sister, you ready for me?"

"Who you calling sister?"

"I call all you women sister."

"I'm too young to be your sister."

"I don't mean it that way. I mean it more in a brotherhood kind of way."

"Oh, like they do down at the Four Square Gospel Tabernacle."

"I wouldn't know about that."

"You don't do church, huh?"

"Not hardly. Too busy working."

"Even on Sunday? I see your boat docked most Sunday mornings."

Shelly tossed a skeptical glance at Bo as she poured fresh coffee into his beat-up mug. She pushed it back across the counter and he slapped the lid on and screwed it down tight.

"Not all fishin' is actually being out fishin'," he growled. "Some of it is gettin' things ready for fishin'."

"Hmm . . . you mean like sleepin' off that Saturday night drunk so you don't fall overboard on Monday morning type of gettin' ready?"

"You're jabberin' about things you know nothing about," Bo bristled. "I don't drink . . . not like that."

He stopped to take a sip and his head jerked back.

"Dang-it . . . that's hot, sister . . . what are you trying to do to me?"

"Wake you up and get you on your way . . . but shuttin' you up would be just as good." She wiped the counter and pretended to be more interested in doing that than talking to him.

"There's no call for that," Bo snapped, mopping his whiskered face with the sleeve of his coveralls. "You just may have seen the last of me." He made sure he made lots of noise as he pushed his way past the tables and chairs toward the door.

Shelly stopped wiping the counter and looked up.

"You know I'm just kidding you? We're just poking at each other. I mean, it's just our way of talking, right?"

Bo stopped and looked at Shelly. He tried to scowl, but Shelly saw the slightest hint of a twinkle in his right eye and that made her smile and then she laughed out loud.

"See you tomorrow, sister."

Bo pushed the door hard to make the bells jangle louder than usual.

Shelly was learning that the harder Bo tried to be the gruff ol' sailor, the softer he became until the twinkle started to show and then he'd deny it and make a fuss and leave so he wouldn't reveal his true self. The reality of it for Shelly was that Bo was as close as she had to any family of any kind—with the exception of Sam, but her relationship with Sam was so one-sided that she wasn't sure if they were really even friends. Bo at least made conversation, and while he sometimes irritated the hell out of her, she understood that at some level they were both just playing roles.

And, Shelly had to cut Bo some slack because he had given the shop its name. She'd already settled on "Shelly's Coffee Stop" but that changed with Bo's dig—"in your dreams"—on that morning when he first burst in while she was getting ready to open. The comment rattled around in her head for the rest of the day and on through the night. But mostly it was that word "dream" that captured her attention, and when she woke the next morning she called the sign shop.

"Hey, Buzz, printed my stuff yet?"

"No, got that on the list for this afternoon."

"Good, because I have a new name. You ready?"

"Sure, go ahead."

"Here it is—Shelly's Dream Bean—in the same font."

"Say that again."

"Shelly's Dream Bean. Got it?"

"Got it. Hey, that's pretty good."

"Thanks."

Shelly thought it was pretty good too, but she would never tell Bo that he had inspired it. She knew that if she did, she'd never hear the end of it.

Chapter 6

Shelly shuddered as the wind rattled the windows of the Dream Bean—not because she was cold but because she knew what that sound meant. She leaned low over the counter to look out across the rooftops and confirm what she had heard: A storm was coming. She straightened up again and looked across her empty shop and knew that storms come in different forms.

September had come and gone with most of the folks in Port Aransas grateful for an above-average tourist season but eager to slow down a little after the summer bustle. There was a pulse and energy during the summer months that was vital to the economy and always exciting at first, but the swelling of the population from around four thousand to as many as sixty thousand wore on the locals after a while. Depending on the weather, everything from the ferry lines to the checkout lanes at the grocery stores were jammed with people. Only the shrimpers, who were in full season and out on their boats, could escape the crush. Still, they were under pressure to pull in nets full of fresh catch for the restaurants that lived and died with the tourist trade.

But if there were sighs of relief as the tourists began to head north to their homes, the fall brought new worries from the south and east. Hurricane season didn't end for another two months, and that put everyone on edge. Port Aransas hadn't taken a direct hit from a hurricane since 1916, but that storm destroyed almost everything. A century later, it was still burned into the communal memory. Nobody wanted to go through that again, especially not Shelly. She'd put everything she had into the Dream Bean, and if she lost that, there was nothing else to lose.

A man like Bo might have been surprised to learn that Shelly was running her own business, but no one was more surprised than Shelly. She never intended to go into business by herself; she got caught up in her father's dream of quitting his welding job in the oil field supply yard and opening an ornamental iron shop.

"You can design the pieces, I'll fabricate them, and your mother can run the office," he said one morning at the breakfast table.

"Me design? What do I know about that, Pop?"

"You've been doodling your whole life. You have a good eye for shapes and dimensions."

Shelly wasn't convinced, but that night when she got home from working her shift at the Crab Cake she pulled her old sketchbooks from a box deep in the back of her closet and flipped through the pages. Her father was right: Drawing had been a passion during grade school and junior high but she lost interest as the teenage years brought their waves of angst and turmoil. And after graduation, the family's finances got tight and she brushed aside the idea of going to college and joined the long line of kids serving food and drinks to the tourists.

But now, with her father's words echoing in her ears, she traced one of her drawings with the tip of her finger and began to remember what it felt like to create. That feeling and her father's dream relit the spark. She started sketching again and enrolled at the community college in Corpus Christi while working as a waitress and hostess at the Crab Cake to pay her tuition. Things were going well until one night when Clarene, the manager, asked her to come back to the office.

"What's up? Did that old fart Franklin complain about his table again?"

Clarene didn't say a word but just kept walking until they got to the door of her office where a state trooper was standing grimly. Clarene pointed them both into her office and closed the door, leaving them together alone.

Shelly's heart pounded in her chest but she didn't know why because she didn't know what the trooper wanted.

"Miss Carson?"

"Uh huh?"

"Miss . . . I'm afraid I have some bad news."

Standing in the hallway, Clarene heard the muffled conversation turn to silence as Shelly learned the news:

Her parents, who had left that morning for a weeklong trip to Shreveport to visit relatives, were just north of Houston when a truck crossed the highway and hit them head on.

As an only child, Shelly was left with everything to settle. The next few weeks were a blur of funeral arrangements and appointments with a lawyer and accountant recommended by the bank. The first thing to fall off Shelly's schedule was school. She rationalized that she needed the time to work on her parents' estate, but the truth was that her interest in a family business died with her parents. She did go back to work at the Crab Cake but mostly out of loyalty to Clarene, because the sad irony of her parents' death was that they left her with plenty to live on.

One night at the Crab Cake when there was a lull in diners, Shelly walked out a side door to get some fresh air. She found Sam sitting on an overturned bucket. He looked at her, nodded, then looked out somewhere into the darkness.

"Slow night," she said.

"Uh huh."

"You're Sam, right?"

"Uh huh."

"You're not from here, are you?"

"No."

"You like it here?"

"Sure."

"Well . . ." The conversation was pointless and Shelly went back inside. As the days went on, however, she started noticing Sam more—the way he did his job and kept to himself. She didn't know anything about him, but what she saw frightened her. She saw a man just going through the motions of living; working to feed himself and to pay rent somewhere, but with life whittled down to little more than that. One night, she asked him where he lived and he said, "A trailer on the beach." And that was it for her. She had to change her ways or risk becoming just like him.

A few afternoons later Shelly was walking near the piers and came upon a small, empty building with a lease sign in the window. She cupped her hands and looked through the glass to see the ghostly remains of a sandwich and sweet shop that had never done well. She turned and looked out from the front and recalled that she had always admired the location: It had a covered porch with a view of the piers, the retail district, and the Gulf out past the rooftops. She called the number on the sign and the next day she leased it. It was pure impulse; she had no plan for what to do there.

But things came into focus a couple of nights later when she and Sam were sitting outside again. They were just sitting quietly, listening to the sounds of the Gulf Coast night, when Sam suddenly spoke.

"I'm sorry."

"About what?"

"Your family."

Shelly was startled. She assumed Sam knew what happened, but she hadn't said anything about it, and he didn't come to the funeral like Clarene and some others at the Crab Cake.

"Thanks. It's been hard, but I'm getting along." She paused. She hadn't told anyone that she had leased the empty shop, but she decided to try it out on Sam. She knew he wouldn't tell anyone else. "I'm leaving the Crab Cake . . . gonna open my own place."

Sam looked over at her and smiled. "That's good."

Shelly exhaled. It was the first time she had said "open my own place" to anyone but the leasing agent, and now that the words had been spoken, it felt very real. Later that night she walked around the retail district and pier area and took note of what was there, and, more precisely, what wasn't there. The next evening she went back to the Crab Cake to give her notice. Clarene took it in stride, giving her a hug and wishing her well. "Just let us know if we can do anything to help you get set up."

Shelly was walking to the front doors when she saw Sam cleaning a table. He looked up at her and she waved. "I'm leaving . . . gonna open a coffee shop near the piers. Come see me sometime."

"Good luck," Sam said.

Shelly opened the Dream Bean a few weeks later. She kept the sandwich shop floor plan, furniture, and fixtures, but she added her own touch by painting murals on the walls and designing her own signs and menu boards. She filled in the rest with what she had seen at coffee shops in Corpus Christi and what she had learned from her months at the Crab Cake. Business was slow at first but picked up as word spread among the locals about the new coffee shop near the piers. Some of the shrimpers even found their way in, especially when the weather kept them off the water. And more than one said that Bo had told them, "Go check out Shelly."

"Was he talking about me, or my shop, because I don't need anyone checking *me* out," she told a group of sailors who came in before sunrise one morning. The men just laughed and let out whistles as they walked out the door. The next time Bo came, Shelly set him straight.

"I appreciate the business, but I don't need you sending the sharks. I'm doing fine all by myself."

"Now, sister, you know I was just sending over some customers. I've got no control over what they want to buy when they get here."

Quicker than lightning Shelly swung the end of her wet rag at Bo's head and knocked his oily cap onto the floor. Bo was startled into silence for a second, but then he burst into laughter as he bent down to retrieve his cap. "I'll let the boys know you're only serving coffee."

As expected, the Dream Bean got a big boost in early June as the tourists began rolling off the ferries with their beach gear and their urban caffeine addictions. Customers eased in and out like the waves on the beach and Shelly was kept busy but never overwhelmed. She began to feel a rhythm that dictated her hours, with the sailors coming in before seven, the locals following at eight, and the tourists floating in at ten. Without any food to offer other than cookies and pastries, noontime was quiet until a little wave of business came around two. After that, she could close the doors and go home unless she sensed that there might be a rogue wave before dinnertime.

Shelly bobbed along through the summer in that way and was beginning to believe she had a better-than-even chance of making it, but then came Labor Day and the tourists packed their cars and headed home. And then the fall storms rolled in and rattled the windows, and hurricane or not, Shelly knew she was sitting in the uneasy eye of having almost no business at all.

Sitting at the kitchen table on a November evening—at the same table where her father shared his dream and launched the journey she now was on—Shelly looked over her finances again. She had enough money to make it through the winter, but she'd need a strong spring break and SandFest to keep her afloat until the tourists came back for the summer. And if they didn't return?

Shelly leaned forward with her palms covering her eyes. To go back to the Crab Cake in defeat with her savings spent was a thought she couldn't bear. She sat up straight and started working the numbers again. "Okay, Pop, I'm not giving up. But . . . I need some help."

Chapter 7

The early morning breeze blew the seashell wind chimes hard against the front window as Shelly turned on the lights and began getting things ready for the day's business. The coffee shop didn't officially open until 7:00 a.m., but Shelly always tried to be there by 6:15 to take care of the few stalwarts that needed a jolt of caffeine to go on their way to their boats or their own businesses. This morning was no different: Bo came through the door right on time at 6:30.

"Hope you're making it strong," he said as he brushed past the tables in his stiff, stained coveralls to the counter, where he plunked down his dented mug. "Gonna be chilly out there for sure."

"Now, Bo, have I ever not made it strong?" Shelly asked as she watched the stream of dark brown liquid tumble into the carafe that she'd positioned under the coffee machine just in time.

"No, but I'm just saying: The wind is whipping up pretty strong even for the first day of winter."

Shelly turned quickly. "Winter . . . is that today?"

"Yep, December 21, just like always. If you'd stop

long enough to check your almanac, or a calendar at least, you'd know what the season is. You'd also know that Christmas is four days away."

"Oh, I'm well aware of that." Shelly nudged the carafe out of the way to fill up Bo's mug. "Shopkeepers have been talking Christmas since Halloween—hoping for a strong year—and they've been decorated since before Thanksgiving."

"All but you. What's your problem? Don't got the spirit?"

"Oh, just haven't got around to it yet. And besides, who are you to be telling me how to run my business? I don't see any Christmas lights strung from your mast out there."

Shelly screwed the lid onto Bo's mug and handed it to him. "Here you go—straight from the beans into your smart mouth."

"Thanks, sister." Bo put a wrinkled dollar bill on the counter. "Keep the change."

"Oh gee, thanks," Shelly said with mock enthusiasm. She knew that Bo knew that the same cup of coffee cost her other customers a dollar fifty. It was written in white chalk on the board above the counter where he stood most mornings.

Bo winked and was headed for the door when Shelly stopped him.

"Hey, have you seen Sam around lately?"

"No, haven't seen him in a week. He's probably holed

up in that tin can of his. These newcomers never know what to do with themselves once the tourists leave and the weather rolls in. See ya."

When only one customer showed up thirty minutes after Shelly turned the Open sign around, she knew it was going to be a quiet day. She was reading the newspaper when Harry came in with the mail.

"Anything interesting today?" she asked, not looking up from her paper.

"Just the usual junk. Looks like you got a few cards." He dug into his large, worn leather bag and pulled out a small bundle bound with a rubber band. "And a letter of some sort from Dallas."

"Oh really?" Shelly set the newspaper aside and slid off her stool to inspect what Harry was placing on the counter. Sure enough, there with the usual offers for cheap auto insurance and steam carpet cleaning were some green and red envelopes embossed with Hallmark on the back and then a white envelope addressed to Shelly's Dream Bean. The return address was in Dallas.

"Need a cup to go?" she asked Harry, noticing that he was lingering in his usual nosy fashion.

"Oh, uh, no, I better keep moving. Wanna finish my route before the rain comes in."

"See you tomorrow then." Shelly watched as he walked out the door and onto the deck and then down to the street.

"Now, let's see," she said to herself as she opened the

white envelope with a utility knife. Inside she found a piece of lined paper wrapped around a smaller envelope. She unfolded the paper and read the handwritten note:

> *Dear Shelly,*
>
> *You may not remember me but I visited your shop in July with your friend Sam. We had an interesting visit while I was there, and I thought maybe he could use a little help. I don't know his address, or even his full name, but I got your address off my receipt from that day and so I'm sending this to Sam by way of you. Please give him the envelope next time you see him.*
> *Sincerely,*
> *Dave*

Shelly thought about it for a moment and then it all came back to her. Sam had come in with that stranger from out of town early one morning in late July. The man, Dave, as she now knew him, bought two cups of coffee—one for himself and one for Sam—and then the two of them sat out on the deck and talked for a while before getting in Dave's car and driving away. She had asked Sam about it when he stopped in the shop a week later but he didn't say much about it—just that he had met Dave on the beach at sunrise that morning. Nothing more.

Shelly tucked the envelope into the pocket of her navy blue apron. Business picked up after that, and she didn't think about it again until late that afternoon when it was time to close. Knowing that it must be something important if it had been mailed by a stranger from Dallas, she decided to drive down the highway and see if she could find Sam. When they worked together at the Crab Cake, they'd talked a little and one of the few things she learned about Sam was that he lived in a trailer just south of town next to a hotel. She'd lived on the island all her life and knew there was just one trailer park that fit that description.

A mile south of town Shelly turned her Volkswagen Beetle off the highway and into the sandy lot that was the trailer park. She got out and walked around, but finding just address numbers and no names on the row of mailboxes near the entrance, she realized she'd never find Sam this way. She certainly wasn't about to go door-to-door and bother people.

Shelly was walking back to her car when she remembered Sam telling her once that he tried to see every sunrise and sunset that he could on the beach. Hearing the breakers just beyond the dunes, she changed direction and walked the short distance to where the hard asphalt gave way to the hard-packed sand. Looking up and down the beach, she saw just a handful of people walking in the hazy light of dusk; then she noticed the silhouette of a man sitting on the ground with his legs crossed.

Sam's mind was empty, his thoughts as invisible as the

wind, when he was startled by the sound of someone calling his name. He stood up quickly and turned to see Shelly, and then, embarrassed by his appearance—ragged shorts and a well-worn long-sleeved shirt—he dusted the sand off his pants and tried to straighten his hair in the wind. He couldn't imagine why Shelly was there, but she didn't keep him waiting to find out. She pulled the envelope from her back pocket and thrust it toward him.

"It's from that man, Dave, who was here last summer. He asked me to forward it to you."

Sam took the envelope and without looking at it he pushed it into his own pocket. "Thanks," he said, and turned back toward the water. Sensing his discomfort at this invasion of privacy, Shelly turned and walked back to her car without saying a word.

Sam lingered as he always did to watch the last light of day kiss the top of the breakers, and then he walked back to his trailer. Inside, he switched on the light and slid onto the built-in bench under the little built-in table. With nervous, unsteady hands he opened the first envelope and read the note that Dave had written to Shelly. Then he opened the smaller envelope and watched as a bank check slid out onto the table. Without touching it, Sam tried to read it from an angle. His eyes fixed first on the name of the account holder—David Shelton—and then the figure handwritten into the amount box. It didn't look right, and he questioned his vision as he reached out and squared the piece of paper on the table in front of him. He read the line that contained his name—simply written as "Sam"—and then the line below, which confirmed the numbers he had seen: "One-hundred and no/hundredths dollars."

The next morning Shelly was waiting on a customer when Sam came in, waited for the transaction to be completed, and then slid the check onto the counter in front of her.

"What am I supposed to do with this?" he whispered nervously.

"Well, Sam, I think you're supposed to do anything you want to with it," Shelly said, and then she caught her breath as she saw the amount. "That's certainly a very generous gift."

"Gift? I don't even know this man."

Sam picked the check up off the counter with an energy and emotion that Shelly had never seen before from this otherwise quiet, gentle man. She watched him pace in front of the counter before walking over to a table, sitting down, and staring out the window at the line of boat masts bobbing above the pier.

The shop was empty, and witnessing Sam's discomfort and confusion, Shelly stepped around the counter and quietly sat down next to him. His weathered hands lay flat on the table with just the pale green corners of the check peeking out. She started to reach out and put her hand on top of his but stopped herself, instead putting a hand on his shoulder just briefly.

"Listen, Sam, I don't know anything about this Dave fellow, and I don't know much about you except for the little you've told me, but it seems to me that you've been given a wonderful gift, pure and simple, and that's the way you should look at it. You can do anything you want to with the check, or you can do nothing at all. It's your choice. Although if you did nothing at all with it, that'd tell me something new about you: that you're a fool. But to be honest, I really don't think that's true at all. Anyway, a check is good for a year, maybe longer, so you can take your time and think about it. I'm sure there's plenty that you need, but that's for you to decide."

Having said all she knew to say, Shelly followed her heart this time and reached down and placed her hand on top of Sam's and gave it a squeeze. She got up to walk back to the counter and heard Sam moving behind her. The jangling of the bells on the door confirmed that he was gone.

Christmas Eve was an especially quiet day at the Dream Bean, and sometime late in the afternoon Shelly noticed that change in the air that people often feel on Christmas Eve—that sensation that it's time to leave the work behind and draw near to family and loved ones. Shelly was alone in town, but she still had that feeling she knew as a girl growing up on the island—when her mother would take off her apron and her father would come home early from the oil field supply yard, and the world would seem to get quiet and watchful.

With thick gray clouds rolling in to hasten the dusk, Shelly began to close down the Dream Bean. She wiped down the tables, swept the floor, and rinsed out the coffee carafes. She soaped and rinsed the last of the utensils from the day's work. She was emptying the cash register and stuffing the contents in a bank bag when she saw a flicker of light out of the corner of her eye. She looked up to see a glow coming from somewhere outside—somewhere up above the store.

Shelly stuffed the bank bag deep under the counter and quietly closed the cash drawer before walking around the counter and across the room to the door. The glow got brighter the closer she got, and leaning forward, she peered upward as she turned the sign to the Closed position. She still couldn't see anything, so she opened the door slowly and stepped out into the moist evening air where she was bathed in a magnificent glow. She backed out across the deck and looked up to see the roofline of her shop perfectly outlined in red, orange, green, and blue Christmas lights. With her mouth hanging open, she backed down the steps to get a better look and saw movement through the railing. She looked closer to see a man kneeling on the deck, tucking a loose electrical cord out of the way. He stood up and turned to face her.

"Sam? What's this . . . ," but before she could complete her question, Bo came bounding into view.

"Well now, Shelly, *this* is what Christmas is supposed to look like." He grabbed her by the hands, spun her once around, and then pulled her back up the steps. "Come on in, sister, and let me buy you a cup of coffee."

Shelly tried to give Sam a wave of "thank you," but Bo pulled her off the porch and into the shop before she could finish the gesture.

Others followed, drawn by the glow of the lights, until the Dream Bean was packed full for the first time since it opened. Shelly kept the coffee perking, and from the oven she brought forth warm cookies and anything else she could find to bake. One of the ladies from a souvenir shop down the block jumped in to help Shelly behind the counter, but nobody took orders or collected cash. Instead, Shelly's tip jar overflowed and then someone put a galvanized bucket on the counter and it filled up too.

Sam kept to himself, letting the others enjoy the party inside while he sat at a table beneath the lights that he had bought and quietly strung the night before. It was cool but not cold, and Sam was comfortable in a new pair of khaki trousers and a long-sleeved shirt. But mostly he was warmed by the glow of the lights and the tall cup of hot coffee that Shelly made sure was never less than half full.

Chapter 8

The new year came as rapidly and predictably as a Gulf Coast squall, with the natives of Mustang Island and the inland plains returning to their routines. The adornments of the holidays were stuffed back into boxes and the boxes back into attics—except at the Dream Bean. Shelly found that Sam's colorful lights provided a festive "Open" sign that could be seen from blocks away on those occasional evenings when she stayed open a little longer. Sometimes that was when something was happening in town, like a play at the community theater, or if a fishing crew was coming in late. And then sometimes she'd stay open late simply because the idea of going home to an empty house was more than she could bear.

Shelly got into the habit of turning on the lights early in the mornings, too, signaling to the crews at the pier and anyone else who wandered by that the door was open and the coffee was brewed. One morning in late January, she had just turned on the Christmas lights, and was sitting behind the counter, working on her budget, when the bells jangled on the front door.

"Come on in. What can I get you?" Shelly said, her eyes still fixed on the notes she was making.

As the customer approached the counter, she slid off her stool, made a final notation, looked up and gasped. Standing in front of her was a middle-aged man with short gray-yellow hair, neatly trimmed and combed with a clean part down the side. His sideburns were well formed, his face cleanly shaved. He wore a denim jacket, a light blue button-down shirt, clean and crisp khakis, and dark brown hiking boots.

"Sam . . . is that *you* in there?"

"Small coffee . . . to go." He shuffled his feet and looked over his shoulder to see if the room was empty.

"Sure thing." Shelly put down her pen and grabbed a cup, but she couldn't curb her curiosity. "So where are you going all brushed up this morning?"

Sam shuffled his feet.

"Well?"

"I have an interview."

"An interview, really? Where?"

"Oh . . . just down at the market. Bagging, stocking, collecting carts, the usual stuff."

"Well that's terrific. Good for you, Sam. Good for you." She popped the plastic lid on the heavy paper cup. "Let me know how it turns out."

"Sure." He counted out the loose change in his hand.

"Oh, don't worry about that. You can pay me when you get your first check."

"Thanks," he said, and poured the change back into his pocket. "See ya."

Shelly watched as Sam turned and walked out the door. Looking back at her notes, she wished that she could offer him a job herself. She would need someone working with her if business ever picked up, but right now margins were still too tight to support anyone but herself. And, Sam didn't have a track record for sticking around anywhere. She couldn't risk him walking away one day when the shop was full. Maybe if he proved himself at the market over the next few months she might have business built up enough to hire someone else and she could steal him away.

~ ~ ~ ~ ~

Sam walked the four blocks to the market, sipping his coffee as he went. He wasn't nervous or anxious as he walked. He didn't think about what questions might be asked or how he might answer them. Instead, he thought about an interview years earlier—not for him, but for a young man who sat across the desk from him at the agency back in Dallas. He had been charged with building a team to handle a new client, and he treated the interview process like he was a king maker.

"So, why do you want to work at Baker & Kimbell? Why do you think you deserve this position over every other green kid who has come through here today?"

The young man, visibly nervous, sat quietly for a

moment while Sam tapped a pen on the desk and checked his watch—actions calculated to throw the young man off. The agency was a fast-paced volatile environment, and Sam was measuring reaction times as much as actual skill and ability. And, he rationalized, it was an initiation that he'd gone through himself so there was no need to hold back on the latest crop of wanabees.

"Well?" Sam said impatiently.

"I guess, I . . ."

"You guess? Listen, son, there's no guessing in this business. No time for it. Clients are waiting for answers, and we have to deliver them quickly, efficiently, and with conviction. They're trusting us with their brand, and they're trusting us with their hard-earned money. If we don't deliver, we all find ourselves sitting right where you are, starting from scratch. So there's no room for hemming and hawing. Either you know who you are and what you have, or you don't."

The young man's face went from pale to bright red in an instant, his eyes narrowed and fixed sharply on Sam, and then he stood up with his portfolio dangling from his left hand, his knuckles white from the grip he had on it.

"Now listen here," he said with a voice that croaked and cracked at first and then settled into a strong, even tone. "I don't need you or anyone else to lecture me on the way an agency operates. I may look young, but I've been doing this work for ten years now. Good work, in fact." He raised his portfolio up shoulder high. "I'm ready to roll up my sleeves and do more good work. But I'm going to be choosy about it. I'm not going to waste my time in an office with people who aren't at least civil to each other. And from what you've shown me, this isn't the kind of place I need to be. Excuse me."

The young man pushed his chair back and walked briskly out the door and down the hall toward the elevators.

Sam, outraged by this eruption of attitude, tossed the young man's resume into the waste basket behind his desk and called out to his administrative assistant, "Trudy, send in the next one."

Eighteen months later that young man, Paul McKenzie, was winning regional Addy Awards at Clark and Shafer. A handful of years after that, his name was on the wall at Clark, Shafer, and McKenzie. And then one day, after the accident that cost him his job and his wife, Sam walked into the lobby of Clark, Shafer, and McKenzie. As fate would have it, his interview was with Paul McKenzie.

"I've been watching you closely. You've done well for yourself," said Sam.

"Only because I've done well for my clients. What was it you told me when I came to interview with you? 'They're trusting us with their brand, and they're trusting us with their hard-earned money.'"

"Did I say that?" Sam struggled to look the younger man in the eye. "Looks like you took it to heart. And I guess that burst of attitude you showed me served you well, too."

"Not really," said Paul. "That was a one-off. I blew up in your office, and then I never did that again. Never needed to. That incident helped me to focus. Ever since then I've trusted my talent, instincts, and determination."

"That's good. Sorry I was so rough on you that day, but it's good to know you used it to good purpose."

Sam looked down at the floor a moment. His shoulders slumped. And then his eyes met Paul's again.

"I wish I could say the same for myself. I've made lots of mistakes, and I know that you know about them. Hard to miss them unless you don't read the trades."

"Yes," Paul said, "and I want to assure you that I'm not going to hold that against you. I know how this business is; I know what it does to people. Still, your work speaks for itself. You're a legend in the business. But . . . our clients are sensitive to these things, so if we were to find a place for you here, we'd have to start you slow and low—out of the spotlight. In a way, you'd be starting over."

"I understand. All I want is a chance . . . which is a lot more than I gave you."

There was another moment of silence. Sam sensed that his time was up, so he stood.

"I brought my portfolio and I can leave it with you." He tapped the side of his slim black case.

"No need. I know your work." Paul stood, too, and

reached out to shake Sam's hand. "I'll be in touch soon."

If Paul kept that promise, Sam never knew it. Forty-eight hours after the interview he was driving to Port Aransas.

~ ~ ~ ~ ~

Just outside the market, Sam dropped his coffee cup into a trash can, checked his reflection in the plate glass window, and pushed through the front doors. He walked to the service desk and to the young woman behind the counter.

"I have an appointment with Ms. Gifford."

The young woman told him to wait a moment, then walked through a metal door. A minute later the doors opened and she directed him to follow her. She led him down a cinderblock hallway to a little room with a time clock and cards on the wall. Inside, he was greeted by Maggie Gifford, a short woman who was clearly ten years younger then he.

"Come in, sit down," she said. "So, I've looked over your resume. You've had a spotty work history here in Port Aransas."

"Yes, ma'am."

"And you've listed nothing before that. Any reason for that?"

"I just didn't think it was relevant. I worked in an office like lots of people, and well, this really isn't an office job."

"That's true, it's not, but it never hurts to brag a little when interviewing. Unless you have something to hide. Do you, Sam?"

He paused for a moment. "No. Like I said, my past experience isn't relevant. That was another place, another time."

"Okay . . . well, I did talk to Clarene at the Crab Cake and she spoke well of you. She said her only disappointment was that you didn't stay very long, and when you left, you just left. Didn't say goodbye or anything. I think it sort of hurt her feelings."

"I'm sorry about that. I didn't leave because of her. I just . . . needed a change."

"I see. Well, here's the deal, Sam. We do have an opening, and I would like to hire you, but there are some expenses for us in getting you set up in the system with your pay and your benefits, and so I need to know that you'll stay awhile. Can you commit to at least six months?"

Sam scratched his head. In his mind, six months seemed like a long time. The former ad man that still occupied a little space in his head told him that six months was longer than the average ad campaign. It seemed like a long time. Still, he did need a steady job. His trailer lease was up for renewal, and there was always the need for groceries.

"Yes, I'll commit to six months."

"Great. The way we do things here is that you'll be on

probation for sixty days, and if it goes well, then we'll extend it out for the entire six months. And then at that time we'll talk again and see about bumping up your responsibilities and your pay."

She stood up and stuck out a hand and Sam did the same.

"You'll start tomorrow morning at nine."

Sam nodded and made his way back down the hallway into the store.

He stepped out into the sunshine and started the walk back down the highway to his trailer. It all sounded reasonable to him—especially the nine o'clock start. That meant he could still start his days on the beach, watching the sunrise.

Chapter 9

Sam spent his first day at the market staying close to Marty, a high school student who had been assigned to show him the ropes.

"It's not a bad gig, Sam," said Marty, talking over whatever was playing in his earphones. "You just have to keep your eyes open and stay on the go. If you keep busy, then you don't have to worry about Gifford putting you somewhere you don't want to be."

Sam followed Marty to the parking lot to gather shopping carts, to the checkout stands to help bag groceries during the mid-morning rush, to the loading dock to roll in fresh produce from the Rio Grande Valley, to the dumpsters with the empty boxes.

During a late-morning break, sitting on the low brick wall in front of the cart station, Sam asked Marty, "This morning you said something about places you don't want to be. Where's that?"

"Oh, that's easy. I don't want to be on the pickle aisle helping put pickle jars on the pickle shelves. I did that once and they started falling off. I thought it'd take all night to clean it up, and longer than that to get the stink out of my clothes." He shook his head in disgust. "Anyway, it's just a job until I get my music going."

Sam looked at Marty and pointed at his earphones. Marty pulled them out of his ears and handed them over to Sam, who put them close to his ears. He was startled, not by the heavy thump of hip-hop or hard metal, but instead the mellow wail of a trumpet.

"Miles?" Sam asked.

"Yeah . . . Miles Davis was the best . . . or at least that's what I think."

"No argument from me," said Sam, a soft smile crossing his face as he handed the earphones back to Marty. "You play the horn?"

"Yeah, but not like that. I'm still building my chops."

"You play in school?"

"Not anymore. That's where I started, but I had to drop out of band. They said I need to work on math and science, even though I don't plan to use any of that."

"So how do you keep learning the horn?"

"I mostly just play by myself. Sometimes I go down to Corpus. There's a couple of groups that let me sit in with them."

"Hmm . . ." Sam turned his face toward the low-hanging sun. The brightness made him squint until he gave in and closed his eyes. He let his mind go blank for a moment until Marty asked him the inevitable question.

"So, what's your story? How come you're not out selling beach houses or doing something like that?"

If only you knew, Sam thought. And then he gave the only answer that made any sense: "I had to drop out too . . . and work on other things."

And before Marty could press him for more details, a voice came from the front doors: "Hey you two, need a little help in here."

The rest of Sam's shift went much the same, making the rounds of odd jobs and chores with Marty until four o'clock came and it was time to punch out and go home. Walking down the highway to the trailer park, Sam thought about Marty and Miles and realized it had been months since he had listened to music with any interest at all. He once took pride in his large collection of vinyl records, but in the fog of the divorce and leaving town, he had left them behind. He wasn't even sure where. He hadn't really cared, until now.

With that thought still in his head, Sam did an about-face on the highway and found his way to Jenny's Memories, a thrift shop stuffed so full that the contents spilled out the front door and onto the parking lot. Most of the stuff outside was either too big or too dilapidated for anyone to steal: bicycles, wheel barrels, washers and dryers, an old Coke machine, the empty shell of a World War II era bomb. Turning sideways to get in the front door, Sam scanned the crowded shelves and aisles until Jenny herself stepped into view. With a tanned face etched by deep wrinkles, short wind-blown gray curls, faded blue jeans, and a red and white plaid flannel shirt with worn-out elbows, Jenny looked like she'd spent a lot of years digging through junkyards and trash heaps.

"What can I help you find?"

Sam's eyes darted about, hoping to land on what he was looking for before he had to ask, but he was hopelessly lost.

"Do you have anything that plays music?"

"Hmm . . . well, let's see." She grasped her chin with her right hand and closed her eyes. She held that pose for ten seconds, and then her eyes opened wide, she let go of her chin, and snapped her fingers. "Back in the corner I have an old brass trombone. Don't know if it still plays but you can give it a try."

"Uh, no, I'm not looking for an instrument to play. I mean, something that I can play music on . . . a CD player or something like that."

"Oh, that's different." Jenny laughed and slapped her leg. "Come on back and let's see what we've got."

Sam followed Jenny as she meandered between stacks of old chairs and shelves of curios, stopping every few paces and placing a finger on her lip as she looked about. They did this several times until she finally let out a "yes sir" and reached down between a drop-leaf table and a red ice chest and pulled out a square brown box with a metal handle. Turning, she shoved it into Sam's arms before he knew what was happening.

"How 'bout this?"

Struggling for a moment to keep from dropping it,

Sam could tell from its shape and the fake leather exterior that it was a portable phonograph from the 1960s.

"Well, that's not exactly what I . . ."

"Of course, you'll need some records too," Jenny interrupted, and while Sam was still trying to form the words "no, thank you," she came back up off the floor with a small stack of LPs. "They're probably a little dusty, but they'll still play."

Sam set the phonograph down on the floor and sorted through the records. A few of them made him wince—Liberace, Steve and Eydie, Pat Boone, The Cowsills—and he was just about to finally tell Jenny "no, thank you" when he came upon the yellowed jacket of an album titled "The Greats of Classical Music."

"You're sure this phonograph still works?" Sam asked, handing all but the one record back to Jenny.

"I'll bet my reputation on it, but if I'm wrong, the trombone is yours for free."

"No, that's okay, I trust you. How much for the phonograph and the record?"

"Ten dollars."

"You take cash?"

"All day, every day."

Jenny led Sam back to the front of the shop and the check-out desk he hadn't seen earlier in all of the clutter. He dug into the pockets of his khakis and pulled out the little wad of cash that remained from Dave's check.

"Come back anytime," said Jenny. "I'll hold the trombone for you."

Sam started back down the highway with the phonograph dangling from his right hand and "The Greats of Classical Music" clutched in his left. Thirty minutes later, back in his trailer, he set the phonograph on the table and opened the lid. Like climbing back on a bicycle, the careful, precise habits of a meticulous audiophile came back to him. With a clean, damp sock, he gently removed the gray ball of lint from the stylus and dusted the rubber surface of the turntable. After rinsing the sock and squeezing out the water, he placed the record on the turntable, switched it on, and, again using the sock, carefully followed the path of the grooves from the outer edge to the cardboard label until the vinyl was shiny and black. When he was certain that the record was dry, he gently lowered the tone arm until the stylus met the vinyl and caught hold of a groove.

As Sam leaned back in his chair, he heard a pop and a hiss and then the first clear notes of Mozart's *Clarinet Concerto in A*. It was, in his long-held opinion, as close as humankind had ever come to creating anything as heavenly as the sound of the ocean kissing the land.

Chapter 10

With each new day at the market, Sam's confidence grew and so did his ease—with other people, and within his own skin. It was as if the tension on a spring inside him was slowly being released, allowing it to relax to its natural state. And like a spring, his moods became more flexible. He was not so dark and quiet. He allowed himself a slight smile, a light chuckle.

Coworkers at the market noticed the change, including Maggie, who knew from watching him that she was wasting Sam's obvious intelligence and maturity on simple chores. Unlike the teenagers in her hire, Sam wasn't distracted by cell phones and mindless chatter. He was focused on whatever he was asked to do. Rather than shove and crash the carts back into the corral where they were kept, Sam rolled them in and carefully made sure that each interlocked with the other for easy removal by the next customer. He was polite and gentle with the customers too, while the kids were loud and rude in the way kids are without even realizing it. Still, Maggie wasn't quite ready to trust Sam completely. He'd been there just three weeks and his work history in town said that he might still walk away at any moment. She couldn't risk having him leave her shorthanded at the checkout stand or during the middle of inventory, so she stuck to her plan to see him through the sixty-day probationary period before trusting him with greater responsibilities.

The one move she did make was to cut Sam free from Marty's umbilical cord after a week. They were doing the same jobs, but their schedules had them in and out of the market at different times. They still sometimes found themselves on the same break schedule and that often led to discussions about music. Sam was fascinated with Marty's interest in music that surely was considered uncool by his peers. In return, Marty pressed Sam for everything he knew about the 1970s and half-seriously chided Sam for his generation's creation of what Marty called "the disco debacle."

"That almost ruined music for all time," Marty said.

Learning that Sam had just one record, Marty invited Sam to meet him at the back of his car after work one afternoon. Marty popped open the trunk to reveal a box full of vinyl records.

"What's all this?" Sam asked.

"Just some old music. Some of it's my parents', some of it's mine. Thought you might want to borrow some."

"Are you sure?" Sam asked as he began thumbing through the albums, revealing a wide selection of artists and genres: jazz, classical, pop, Motown, rock 'n' roll.

"I'm sure. My parents don't play them anymore, and I've downloaded a lot," he said, patting his ever-present iPod in his shirt pocket. "Go ahead."

Sam picked out a half-dozen of the records and slid them into a fabric grocery bag for the walk home.

"Thanks again," Sam said over his shoulder as he walked away, "and don't leave those in the trunk. They'll warp in the heat."

"I'm young, but I ain't dumb," Marty shouted back.

Nobody was more aware of Sam's change than Shelly, who'd first known him as a near-mute dishwasher and beach bum. She tried not to make a big deal of it in his presence, because she knew that too much attention might set Sam back. He was still prone to shyness, and he might withdraw completely if she gushed over him too much. So, she just went along with the change and, as Sam showed more of himself, she upgraded the level of their conversations, drawing him out a little bit more. And Sam was showing up more frequently too, stopping for a cup of coffee on his way to work. It was a nice counterbalance to Bo's early morning visits. While Bo often put her on edge, Sam's calm, gentle manner put her at ease.

One chilly morning in late February, two worlds collided when Sam arrived a full hour early, and Bo came in an hour-and-a-half late.

"What are you doing here so early?" Shelly asked Sam. "Did Maggie change your hours?"

"No, gonna stop by the bank."

"Not to rob it, I hope."

"No, the opposite. I'm gonna open an account."

"Gosh, I thought you'd have done that months ago."

"Hadn't really needed one till now."

"Good for you. Maybe that means you're going to stick around?"

Shelly handed Sam his cup. She waited for an answer but Sam just smiled and stepped down the counter to get a lid and some napkins. From behind him the door jangled.

"Hey, sister, ready for me?" Bo boomed as he entered the shop.

Shelly looked at the clock on the wall. "Where've you been?" she said with mock concern. "Thought maybe you fell in the channel."

"Not a chance. That only happens to you shore huggers. You step off a pier and then men like me have to come fish you out. Oughta just let you fend for yourself. The island's gettin' a little crowded anyway."

"That's a little harsh, don't you think," Sam said quietly, avoiding eye contact.

Bo looked at Sam, then at Shelly, then back at Sam.

"See you later," Sam said to Shelly and turned and walked out the door.

"Who the hell was that?" Bo asked as he watched Sam step down off the deck and walk away down the sidewalk.

"Sam."

"Sam? You mean Trailer Park Sam? That Sam?"

"Yes, Bo, that Sam," said Shelly, irritated.

"Did he win the lottery or something?"

"No, nothing so dramatic. He's just getting himself together a little."

"My, oh my. I wouldn't have recognized him. Heck, I didn't even think he knew how to talk. And when he did . . . a little protective, if you ask me."

"Nobody's asking you," Shelly snapped.

"It wouldn't hurt you any," said Bo.

"What's that?" said Shelly, her irritation growing.

"Having someone look after you."

"I thought that's what you keep coming in here for, telling me how to run my business and everything?"

"You know what I mean."

"Oh, so now you're an expert on that too."

"I know some things," Bo said, and then he started walking toward the door.

"You know what I just realized?" said Shelly as Bo stopped to take a sip of coffee before reaching for the door. "Despite all our back and forth every day for all these months, I don't know anything about you."

Bo wiped his mouth on his sleeve. "There's nothing to know," he said, and he was gone.

Shelly wiped the counter, but not because it was dirty. It was becoming a nervous habit; she wasn't even sure what she was nervous about except that something inside her was telling her that life was getting complicated. Sam, Bo, that Dave guy from Dallas—the Dream Bean was becoming a haven for misfits. She'd have been happy just to have a steady run of strangers who wanted coffee and left her alone.

Chapter 11

As Sam sat on a worn sofa in the bank lobby, waiting to open an account, he held a firm grip on the two checks representing four weeks of steady work at the market. It had been years since he had been inside a bank, thanks to his high-paying agency job and the convenience of direct deposit. In the months since he'd arrived in Port Aransas, he cashed the occasional check at one of the convenience stores willing to do his banking in exchange for a small percentage. But now, here he was at a bank, waiting his turn with hourly workers like himself and old coots who insisted on touching and feeling their social security checks before handing them over to a living, breathing teller. Sam knew from the chatter that these transactions were as much social as they were financial.

"How're you doing today, Miss Ida?"

"Oh, just fine."

"Whatdaya hear from the grandkids?"

"Oh, little Susie is giving her momma fits as usual, wanting to be carted around here and there."

"I know that's true. These kids just wanna be going all the time. You want a hundred in twenties like usual?"

"Yes, sweetie, that'll be fine . . ."

As the chatter floated in and out of his ears, Sam's dozy mind began to focus on fragments of conversation from another corner of the room.

"I just think that's so exciting. We've finally arrived if they're looking at moving in here."

"Yeah, but it's not going to be so good for everyone. That Shelly down by the docks—she's just getting started. She's already gone through so much, and now this. She's gonna have a fight on her hands for sure."

"That's the way it goes. Bigmart came in and pushed out Smith's, and now most of the family is working there. I hear they're doing fine, running some of the departments and all."

"I know, but I still don't like it none."

Sam turned slightly to see who was talking when a young woman in a dark, ill-fitting business suit walked up.

"If you'll follow me, we'll get you set up."

Sam followed her to a cubicle, and thirty minutes later he had an account number and a temporary checkbook. Stepping out onto the sidewalk, he stopped for a moment to think. What he needed to do was to get down the street to the market and start his shift, but what he wanted to do was walk the opposite direction to the Dream Bean. Halfway to the market, he wheeled around. "Dammit."

Shelly was getting ready for the noon rush when Sam

pushed open the door of the Dream Bean, panting hard.

"Sam, what's happened?" Shelly asked.

"Nothing . . . at least not yet."

"What do you mean, Sam? What's going on?"

Sam plopped down at a table to catch his breath. Shelly came from behind the counter and sat at the table next to him.

"Okay," she said, leaning forward and putting a motherly hand on top of his, "What's up?"

As Sam told her what he'd heard, and what he thought it meant, Shelly pulled away and clasped her hands together.

"So you're telling me one of the national coffeehouses is coming to town?"

"Yes . . . maybe even Sea Siren . . . and if they are . . . you need to be ready."

"What do you mean 'be ready'? I'm already here. I'm open for business. What else is there to do?"

"It's not enough just to be open." Sam spoke slowly, his breath finally catching up with his words. "You have to be memorable. You have to be the favorite. You have to be the best."

Shelly stared at Sam in disbelief. He started to say more but she put her hand up to stop him. "What? . . . Huh? . . . Where is this coming from all of a sudden?" She stood up, her voice growing louder, her tone sharper. "Furthermore, what business is it of yours? In fact, what right do you have to come in here and tell me how to run my business . . . you, who can't hold a job for more than a few weeks? It seems to me like you have more than enough to work on in your own sorry life without poking your nose into mine."

By the time she'd finished talking, she was behind the counter with her back to Sam, wiping down the coffee machine in her nervous way.

Embarrassed, Sam looked at the floor until Shelly, without turning to face him, said, "Well, what are you still doing here? Get on out of here and go do whatever you bums do on your day off."

Sam left in silence, stung. He was angry, but not at Shelly. He knew he had gone too far, and he was baffled by what had just happened. Where did all that opinion come from, and who was he to be telling anyone else what to do? He was, after all, exactly what Shelly had called him: a bum. And on top of that, why did he care at all what happened to Shelly or the Dream Bean or anyone else on the island? That last thought was running through his head as he walked into the trailer park and pushed open the unlocked door of his trailer. Sitting down on the bed and leaning forward to rub his face, he felt the weight of his nametag from the market in his shirt pocket and realized he had forgotten to go to work. "Just as well," he thought. "They expect me to fail."

Back at the Dream Bean, Shelly's anger boiled over.

"Not now, not in my town!" she roared, pacing back and forth in front of the counter in the now frighteningly empty coffee shop. She'd worked too hard and come too far to see the Dream Bean run out of business by outsiders with a familiar sign and endless cash. She knew the locals might keep coming, but the tourists would line up out the door at a shop with the same hours and menu as the shop at the end of their own street back home.

Shelly managed to get herself under control before the lunch crowd arrived, but as she looked into the faces of the women and men who came to her counter—many who had become regulars—she fought back the tears and the fear. She knew that Sam was right: She could lose everything. Later, when the Dream Bean was empty again, the silence overwhelmed her. All of her wiping couldn't keep the counter dry as tears dripped from her swollen eyes. She hadn't cried since she'd buried her parents, and the salty tears came now as if she'd been storing up seawater inside her head.

Chapter 12

When Shelly arrived at the Dream Bean the next morning, Bo was sitting on the front steps.

"Where you been?" He yawned and wiped his face with his leathery hand.

"What's it to you?"

"Well now, I knew you had some attitude here at the shop, but I didn't know you brought it from home."

Shelly said nothing as she walked past him and unlocked the door. She walked through the dark shop and disappeared down the hallway. Bo waited just inside the front door until the lights blinked on and Shelly came back out and began her morning prep as if nobody was there.

For all his pretending to care about nothing but himself and his boat, Bo could tell when something was amiss and knew when to keep his mouth shut. He sat down at a table in the middle of the room and only when he heard the coffee machine quiet from a loud gurgle to a hiss did he step up and set his mug on the counter. Shelly picked it up, filled it, and set it back down next to the two dollars Bo had placed on the counter.

"Thank you," he said, and followed with, "Have a nice day," as he walked to the door. Shelly was in the back room by then and didn't hear him.

Miles away, Sam awoke to the sound of seagulls and the gritty feeling of sand in the corner of his mouth. Raising his head, his shoulders, and then his torso, he looked around for a moment and then the events of the past twenty hours came back into focus. After the confrontation with Shelly, he went back to the trailer and decided to blow off work and then decided to hustle in. But halfway into town he changed his mind and went back to the trailer with the intent to pack up and leave town. He started gathering up his stuff and realized that not only did he have no idea where he would go, but he also had no way to get there other than with his two feet or the rusty bicycle that lay in the weeds. Changing his mind again, he got out of his work clothes and into his shorts and T-shirt to walk the beach. With his bare feet in the sand, he remembered a childhood visit to South Padre Island when he wondered how long it would take to walk the shoreline to Mexico. With that thought in his mind, Sam started walking south and when the sun set, he walked up into the dunes to sleep.

Now, judging from the growing light and the pink and orange foam on top of the breakers, Sam knew it was about 6:30 in the morning. He stood up, stretched, dusted himself off, and walked down to the water where he washed the dried sand off his face and ran his wet fingers through his tangled hair until it lay flat on his scalp. Feeling the sharp pain from his full bladder, he walked back up into the dunes and relieved himself.

Turning left, Sam began to walk north up the beach and was surprised at how far he had come the afternoon before. For three hours he walked—the ocean on his right and expanses of dunes and tall coastal grasses on his left—until he began to see rooftops and signs on the coastal highway and then the golf course on the edge of town. And that's when it struck him how he had completely dismissed the notion from the night before that he would walk more than a hundred miles down the coast to Mexico. He shook his head; he was neither a bold adventurer nor an aimless bum. He was just a man walking back to what he had come to know as home.

Back at the Dream Bean, the phone rang and Shelly answered it to find Maggie from the market on the other end of the line.

"Hi Shelly, have you seen Sam recently?"

"No."

"He didn't come to work yesterday and I thought maybe you'd seen him."

"No, I haven't."

"Well, someone said that you might have seen him because he and you . . ."

"They'd be wrong about that," Shelly interrupted. "He comes by every now and then for coffee, but so do lots of other folks."

"Well, I just thought . . ."

"Listen, I don't have time to keep up with Sam or anyone else. Gotta go. Bye." Shelly put the phone down. "The nerve."

~ ~ ~ ~ ~

In Dallas, Dave leaned against the wall of the crowded commuter train and closed his eyes. He learned years ago that it was best to avoid eye contact if he didn't want to get pulled into the petty conversations and dramas of others. But now he was aware that his own life had become the bland tableau of what he had always imagined as the life of others: commute, work, commute, dinner, sleep, alarm clock, repeat. At least when Debby was fighting the cancer their lives had meaning. Every day had an agenda, and everything they did—from the stress of doctor appointments to the ordinary choosing of what and where to eat dinner—was faced with determination and purpose. His fellow commuters might have been facing a difficult meeting or a showdown with a manager, but he and Debby had been fighting for their lives. Every sunrise was cherished. Every breath was a gift. Every tender moment was absorbed and written on their hearts. Now, when Dave looked across the train at the frozen mask of another commuter, he knew he was gazing at a mirror.

He'd been patient and done as advised; he'd resisted the temptation to head for the hills and instead maintained the status quo. But what his accountant and friends didn't understand was that the status quo for twenty-five years had included Debby—in health and in sickness, as their vows had dictated. Now, without her, there was no status quo. It was as if he had been living in a play and the familiar backdrop had suddenly been lifted out of sight and replaced with a blank white canvas. With nothing familiar but a few pieces of stage setting—a chair, a desk, a bed—the question before him now was: how would he paint the backdrop, if at all?

These were the questions that flowed constantly through Dave's mind once grief had subsided and intense loneliness had been replaced by passive solitude. He was in a place where he functioned well at everything he needed to do, but there was a pervasive interior conversation going on inside his head. He knew the voices well, and while one made lists, the other said, "Screw it, just do it man." And the thing he was grappling with now was the urge to "just do it." Was it a safe plan to rebuild a life out of the pieces that were left behind by Debby's death? Or was it a complete and total overhaul of everything he was and everything he knew about himself?

By the time the train stopped at Akard Station, Dave had a headache from thinking so hard about these things. He knew some of that was because he hadn't had his coffee yet—his one true addiction—and so in his usual manner he walked to his cubicle, hung up his jacket, turned on the computer, and walked down the hall to the coffee machine while his computer booted up. When he returned, he dropped into his chair with a heavy sigh and started checking morning email and his calendar, which showed a marketing meeting at 9:30 a.m. Looking at the clock, it was 9 a.m., and with not enough time to really get started on anything fresh, he jumped onto the internet and checked the news.

Thirty minutes later, Dave and his colleagues learned that the company was contracting with an outside agency to freshen their image a little. There were the usual expressions of concern from middle managers who were afraid of losing control, but the vice president assured them that everything was okay.

"Don't worry about that. We're going to have checks and balances at every decision point," he said. "Besides, if anyone has a right to feel threatened, it's me, because I'm the leader of this group and the agency is taking on a piece of my domain. But I'm swamped with other programs right now so I look at it as welcome help where we need it. Now," he said, standing up and sliding brochures down the table, "I want you to read up on these folks so you'll know who the players are. You'll all be interfacing with them at different times."

Dave reached into the middle of the table and grabbed a brochure as he stood up to leave. The meeting was over and the managers disappeared down the hallways. Some walked away in pairs to continue their conversations about this invasion of outsiders, but Dave just shrugged it off. He didn't care one way or the other. The brochure joined one of the piles on his desk and didn't get any more attention till later in the afternoon when Johnny, a writer in the group, stepped into Dave's cubicle.

"I hear we're being replaced," he said, with a mixed look of fear, resentment, defensiveness, and disdain.

"No . . . no . . . not replaced," Dave said. "Just . . . augmented."

"Well, they wouldn't be doing this if they thought we could do it ourselves. You know we're already stretched so far . . ."

"And that's why they're bringing in outside help," Dave said calmly. "They know you already have a full plate."

"Well it feels like they don't trust us or something."

"Listen, I've been in this situation before, and the best thing you can do is appreciate the fact that you have more time to concentrate on your main job. Besides, this is the way it's going to be, so you can either go along with it or go somewhere else."

Johnny looked at Dave, and seeing the calm in the eyes of this man who was fifteen years older and had more experience, he relaxed a little, enough to uncross his arms.

"Okay, so who are these people?"

"Here," Dave said, and handed Johnny the brochure.

"A brochure . . . really? That's so old school," Johnny said, adding an air of superiority to his tone as he thumbed quickly through the pages. "We'll see." He handed the brochure back to Dave and walked away.

Dave leaned back in his chair and looked at the brochure for the first time. There was nothing especially interesting or distinctive on the pages, but seeing the web address printed on the back, he swiveled his chair to face his computer. "More research" he told himself. As he clicked on link after link, he found a list of the agency's clients, samples of print and video campaigns, and a short history. Scrolling through a timeline that began in 1983, his eyes fell on a typical grip-and-grin image of three men with a crystal trophy. The caption read, "2007 Addy Awards." Dave scrolled down the page and his eyes fell on one of the three—a handsome man with wavy blond hair and a confident smile. But it wasn't the smile that caught his attention. It was the look in his eye.

Dave sat up straight in his chair and went into hard-core research mode. He jumped onto the website of the Dallas Ad League and found a link to the Addy Awards and then a list of 2007 winners. There, he found the name of the agency that his firm had just hired, and the winners of the award for Best Print Campaign. Listed among the three winners was Sam Barnes.

"No way," Dave said out loud. He checked his calendar, logged himself out for Thursday and Friday, and booked a room at the hotel in Port Aransas.

Chapter 13

Three days went by with no sign of Sam at the market or the Dream Bean. Maggie checked her manual for the rules on job abandonment, then she walked into the break room, pulled Sam's time card out of the rack, and tossed it in the trash. "Rules are rules," she said.

That afternoon Marty stopped by the Dream Bean to ask about Sam.

"I don't know where he is or what he's been doing," Shelly said. "What's it to you?"

"I worked with him at the market. He got fired."

"Oh yeah? What'd he do this time?"

"He hasn't shown up in days. Didn't even call in."

"Well, considering he doesn't have a phone, that part of it makes sense. So why are you looking for him now?"

"Just wanted to check on him. I'm a little worried about him, I guess."

"Well there's no need to be," Shelly said gruffly. "He's a grown man and he's old enough to make his own mistakes."

"Still . . . do you know where he lives?"

"Down at the trailer park. I don't know . . ."

"Thanks," Marty said, and walked out the door.

"Good luck without a number," Shelly said out loud.

But Marty didn't need the trailer number. When he got out of his car at the trailer park he heard music, and as he followed it to the door of an especially rusty old trailer, he recognized the jaunty five-four rhythm of the Dave Brubeck Quartet coming from an open window. He knocked on the door, and when nobody answered, he knocked again and rattled the handle. He heard the shuffle of feet, and then the door opened about six inches to reveal Sam. He scratched his scraggly head in a silent attempt to question the interruption.

"Hey Sam," Marty said.

Sam said nothing but opened the door and stepped outside. He sat down on the rusty step and looked up at Marty through bleary eyes.

"You're playing Brubeck," Marty said.

"Uh-huh," Sam said softly.

There was a long pause and Marty understood that Sam wasn't going to say anything else.

"So . . . we missed you at the market, and I guess you know that, well, Gifford fired you."

"Didn't know that, but not surprised."

Marty shuffled his feet in the sand, not sure what to say next.

Finally, "What'll you do?"

"Pretty much what I'm doing now, which is what I was doing before."

"You need anything?"

"Naw, I'll be alright, kid. Appreciate you coming by."

Understanding that the conversation was over, Marty moved backward a step and was turning to go when Sam spoke.

"Tell Ms. Gifford I appreciate the work . . . and I'm sorry for leaving without letting her know."

Marty nodded and walked toward the wooden fence, but before he got to the gate he stopped and turned. "Man, you're one messed up dude."

Sam looked down at his own bare feet and waited for the sound of tires rolling away on loose gravel before standing up. Stretching for a moment, he looked past the gate and the fence toward the hotel and saw a man getting out of his car with a small duffle bag. When the man turned and looked toward the trailer park, Sam rushed up the steps and slammed the door.

Chapter 14

Dave parked in front of the Dream Bean and dashed up the steps. He jerked the door open so hard that even Shelly was startled by the clatter of the bells—but not as much as she was by the sight of Dave walking swiftly across her floor. She brushed back her long hair with her free hand, fearing that she looked a mess. That response was triggered a millisecond earlier by the realization that this mysterious young man named Dave—the one who had sent a check to Sam through her—was looking a lot more polished and handsome than he had when she saw him for the first and only time in July.

"Good morning," he said. "I need two coffees to go."

"You're Dave, right?" Shelly pulled up two tall cardboard cups. Of course, she knew the answer, but it seemed to be the thing to say since they'd only met that one time before.

"Yes, and you are Shelly. Good to see you again." He smiled.

"What brings you back to Port A?"

"Oh, just taking some time off."

"Got someone with you?"

Shelly stole a glance out toward the porch as she filled the two cups.

"No, on my own. Actually, I was hoping to see Sam again. Thought he might like another cup of coffee."

Shelly slid the two cups toward Dave, and as he snapped the lids on, he glanced over his shoulder—there were just a few customers—and leaned forward against the counter as if to share a secret. Reading his body language, Shelly leaned closer toward him, her eyebrows arching.

"You know . . . Sam . . . he isn't who we think he is." Dave paused. "I mean, he isn't *what* we think he is."

"And what do we think he is?" Shelly asked.

"Well . . . we think he's just a shiftless man from nowhere who lives in a trailer."

"He does live in a trailer, and as of earlier this week he is unemployed again. Actually, he made a go of improvement for a few months, and he has you to thank for that."

"Me?"

"Yes. That check you sent him last December? That got him going in a new direction, and for a while it looked like he was starting to turn his life around. He cleaned himself up, bought me some Christmas lights, got a steady job, and he started saying more than two words, but then he . . . ."

Shelly stopped in mid-sentence, the truth of what had happened finally becoming clear to her.

"Oh my . . . that poor man . . . I've done this to him." She covered her mouth as tears welled up in her eyes. "He was just trying . . ."

"What . . . what happened?"

"We got into an argument, and I ran him off." Shelly sighed heavily, and then she recounted the conversation with Sam about the threat to her business.

"I shouldn't have taken it out on him. He seemed to know what he was talking about, and it scared me and I didn't want to listen to him."

"That's just it," Dave said. "He *did* know what he was talking about. That's what I'm trying to explain. He wasn't always like he is now. He's coming back . . . from something bad. I can't quite piece it together. That's what I want to see him about."

Shelly listened and took it all in. Her fears about the shop were now replaced with concern for Sam. She knew how sensitive he was, and she feared now that pressure from Dave might push him even further away.

Finally, she spoke. "Why do you need to bother him about it?"

"I don't need to bother him at all. I just . . . I just want to know him better." Then he took a long pause. "Shelly, Sam is a good man. He's done some great things. He can do great things again if he wants to."

"Well that's just it: What if he doesn't want to do anything else? What if he just wants to be left alone?"

Dave stared at Shelly, frustrated. He was driven by

compassion, but also by a riddle. What had happened to turn the brilliant, dashing man in the photo into a sad loner? And what could he do to help bring him back? He had to know. He was about to say that but Shelly spoke.

"Do you need me to go with you?"

"No, I know how to find him."

"Then make me a promise."

"What?" he asked, his frustration growing.

"Don't push him too hard, okay?"

"I won't." Dave reached across the counter and gave Shelly's hand a squeeze and then grabbed the coffee cups and hurried out the door.

Down on the beach, the sun was losing its battle with the afternoon clouds that drifted in off the water. Gulls picked at shells and debris that had washed onto the sand, but the tourists were all gone, having drifted inland to the hotels and restaurants. Dave stood at the edge of the beach road and took a sip from the cup in his right hand, the coffee still warm. The full cup in his left hand was beginning to feel heavy and he thought about walking it over to the trashcan when he saw movement out of the corner of his eye. He squinted and just on the thin edge where the brown-gray sand meets the blue-gray sky, he saw the silhouette of a man walking.

Dave looked around and spotted a beach shower. He walked over, sat on the edge of the wooden platform, and waited. As he watched Sam approach, he tried to calculate the perfect distance from which to make his presence known—not so far as to need to shout, and not so close as to startle him. His eyes found a clump of seaweed, and when Sam reached that point, Dave spoke.

"Hey there."

Sam turned and looked, and when he saw Dave, he stopped walking.

"Coffee?" Dave raised the cup in his left hand.

Sam looked up the beach to see if anyone was looking. He wiped his mouth on the back of his hand, shrugged a little, and walked slowly toward Dave, who reached upward and handed him the cup.

"I thought I saw you earlier going into the hotel," Sam said quietly, still standing. "On vacation?"

"No." Dave took a long pause, knowing this was his chance. "Actually . . . I came to see you."

Sam's shoulders tightened. "Really. What about?"

"You . . . and, well . . . the past."

"How do you mean?"

"It's just . . . I saw your picture in a brochure. I Googled you . . . and . . . I learned a few things."

"I'm sure you did."

"I learned that you were once one of the leading art directors in Dallas, in the Southwest in fact, and . . . ." He was going to say more, but he stopped.

Sam sat down beside Dave, took a long sip from the coffee cup, and then without any prompting he started talking. Slowly, quietly, with full detail and perfect recall, he told his story as if it had all just happened.

Chapter 15

The launch of the new campaign was a throwback to the mid-1980s when everything worth doing in Dallas was done big. When a skyscraper topped out, they had a huge party from the lobby to the penthouse with free-flowing booze and food, and big-name entertainment. When Fountain Place opened, the party featured New Orleans jazz clarinetist Pete Fountain. Down the street at Lincoln Plaza, it was Ray Charles. The parties died when the boom turned to bust, and after that, when a new building or business opened, it was strictly low key. Fiscal responsibility became the sign of maturity and success.

But things were different in 2010, and when it was time to debut the campaign for the new steakhouse, Sam decided it was time to put some fun back into doing business. He had no problem convincing the client that the money for a party would come back to them multifold in new customers.

When it came time to plan the party, Sam knew exactly who he wanted to put it all together. Kayla was young, vivacious, and fresh out of college with bright ideas. She'd taken an average communications position and transformed it into a profit driver by harnessing the power of social media. The days of press releases were over; Facebook and Twitter were what got people's attention now, and Kayla was using them to draw people to restaurants and retailers that the agency represented. When Sam told her he wanted her to plan the party from start to finish, she jumped in with gusto.

And under Kayla's direction it all came together spectacularly. A couple of hundred people crowded into the starched white tent at the site of the new restaurant to sample fare from the menu, listen to live music and, of course, drink from the well-stocked bars at each corner. Except for an intermission when the clients welcomed their guests and promised more of the same great food when the restaurant opened, it was non-stop revelry.

Close to midnight, Sam was talking to one of the guests when Kayla walked up.

"Hey Kayla, you've done a wonderful job here. I knew you would. We're going to do more of these parties, so you need to start making plans for the . . ."

"Oh . . . sure, that's great. I love doing this," she said. "But, I need to get home. Last train leaves in a little while. I've closed things out with the wait staff and the band and they'll pack up on their own."

"What, you're not staying till the end? Come on now, just another hour. What can it hurt? Call Bill . . ."

"It's Bob," she interrupted.

"Right, well call him and tell him you'll be home soon. You don't need to take the train. I'll give you a ride. In fact, when I get in tomorrow I'm going to see what we can do about getting you a parking space so you don't have to ride the train anymore."

"Okay," she said, still a little uncertain.

An hour later, she was in the passenger seat of Sam's Mercedes as they curved northward up Turtle Creek Boulevard. Sam was driving and checking email when his right tires bumped the curb and popped the cell phone out of his hand. Reaching out to catch it as it bounced off the console, he lost control, jumped the curb completely and plowed into a large oak tree. The airbags deployed, but that didn't keep Kayla's body from slamming against the door and the window.

The next thing that Sam was aware of was a flashlight shining in his face. He heard noise to his right and looked over to see a paramedic attending to Kayla.

"This way, sir," a voice said, and Sam turned to see another paramedic reaching his hand in to help him out of the driver's seat.

The rest was a fog of sensory stimulation: lights in the eyes, questions, cold steel on his wrists, the odor of dirty vinyl, muffled conversation, the backs of heads and the glow of a monitor, a wobbly walk down a long hallway, more questions, a hard bench, a sweaty mattress.

Around seven in the morning, Sam awakened to the sound of his own name. "Time to go," said a uniformed officer, who opened the door and led Sam back down a hallway to a desk where Brenda was waiting. Sam noticed that she looked beautiful as always, but in her eyes he could see fatigue and anger.

"Come on," she said tersely, thrusting a heavy paper envelope into his hand. He knew from the sound and feel of it that it contained his wallet, keys, watch, phone. It wasn't until he got into the car that he noticed his shoelaces and belt were in there too.

They rode home to North Dallas in silence, Sam's head aching. He knew from Brenda's body language that she was totally pissed at him. And he knew from living with her for twenty-five years that he shouldn't say a word. Best thing was to go home, get cleaned up, and then slowly ease into the appropriate expressions of sorrow and remorse. After all, he'd never had an accident before, and while it was true that he'd been drinking, it was really the distraction of the cell phone that caused the crash.

And just as he was thinking about how he would make his case, he recalled that Kayla had been with him. He was mulling that over when a new crisis presented itself: As they came around the corner and drove the half-block to their house, Sam saw two TV trucks parked in front. It was eight and the morning shows had set up their cameras to broadcast live. Sam groaned.

Brenda put her head down and turned the car past the media and curious neighbors and onto the driveway and down the side of the house and into the garage. Watching in her rearview mirror, she pushed the button that closed the garage door. She got out of the car quickly and left Sam behind. When he got inside the house, the doorbell was ringing.

Sam started to say something but Brenda stopped him.

"Don't you dare open that door."

Sam said nothing and did as he was told. He and Brenda got through the rest of the day without saying a word to anyone, or to each other.

Late that night, after Brenda had gone to bed, Sam checked the newspaper online and was disturbed to see his mug shot on the home page with the details of the crash, including what he did not know: Kayla was hospitalized with a concussion, scrapes, and bruises; her parents had rushed to Dallas from Tennessee; and they'd brought a lawyer with them.

Sam checked his office email and found instructions to stay home for a few days. "Come back at 7 a.m. on Monday. We'll discuss the future then."

Monday morning, Sam found the hallways empty and quiet—not unusual for that hour—but when he got to his office, he understood the timing of his arrival. On his desk was a neatly sealed box, and on top of that was a large envelope. He opened it to find the details of his separation from the agency: his final paycheck, a severance check, a packet on outplacement services and interim health insurance coverage. On top of it all was a brief letter from the **HR** manager thanking Sam for his service, explaining that the rest of his personal belongings would be delivered to him in a few days, and answering his only question: There would be no negotiating his return.

Somewhere inside of Sam the remnants of dignity found light. He lifted the box and envelope, checked the hallway, and hastily walked down the hall, out the door, and climbed into the plain sedan he had rented over the weekend. As he drove away, he looked in the rearview mirror and let out a sigh. Nobody had seen him.

As Sam drove home, it felt like the world was moving in slow motion. But that was a wicked deception because when he got home he found that things were moving fast.

When Sam walked into the kitchen with the box in his hands, Brenda didn't have to ask what had happened at the office. She had expected it.

"I need time to think things through," she said without emotion.

"Think what through? I made a mistake. One really bad mistake. I'm sorry I've embarrassed you."

"Oh, you've not really embarrassed me; I think you've embarrassed the hell out of yourself and the agency."

"Come on now," Sam said, "if they're embarrassed, it oughta be because they've jumped to conclusions."

"Well you gave them plenty of reason," Brenda said. "And what about that poor girl?"

"She'll be fine. Just some bumps and bruises."

"What about her reputation?"

"Wait a minute, you don't think that she and I . . ."

"I don't know what I think at this point. Besides . . ."

"Besides what?"

"Oh . . . nothing . . . I just need time to sort through it, and I can't do that with you here."

"What are you saying?"

"I think we need some space. I need some space."

"Are you leaving?"

Brenda glared at Sam.

"Oh, I see, you're wanting *me* to leave," Sam said.

For all of his bravado at the agency, Sam wasn't a fighter at home. He spent the rest of the day packing his car with clothing and files and other things he would need to launch a job search and ultimately his comeback. He wasn't going to let one bad night define him. He wasn't going to live in the shadow of rumors and innuendo either, so when he drove away from the house he headed south through town, across the river to Oak Cliff, where he found a small, furnished apartment to rent.

A few days later, Sam found a large manila envelope crammed into the apartment mailbox. Inside were divorce papers citing "irreconcilable differences." Sam was stunned—"think things through," Brenda had said—but he wasn't deterred. He'd show Brenda and the rest of the world what he was made of.

Sitting on a hard, wooden chair in the middle of the little den, Sam sorted through the stack of files he had quickly pulled from the file cabinet at the house. It had been years since he'd compiled a portfolio, and doing so now had him looking back over the remnants of past campaigns and glory. But advertising changes with the culture, and while some of what he saw still filled him with pride, a lot of it made him cringe. And some of it he had completely forgotten about over the years.

Still, he pulled together a portfolio, and after a few days on the phone, he found himself in the office of Clark, Shafer, and McKenzie, sitting across the desk from Paul McKenzie who he had bullied years earlier.

Afterward, back in the quiet of his apartment and feeling hopeful but chastened by the idea of "starting over," Sam returned to sorting through his files. He made two piles on the floor—material to keep, and trash to throw away. Working through the files he came upon mementos from his life outside of the office: early resumes and college transcripts, instruction manuals for appliances long gone, the lease contract from a rent house, and the homeowner rules from the tiny condo he and Brenda bought and sold back in the eighties.

Sam opened an envelope and caught his breath. Inside was the appraisal document for the loose diamond that he bought for Brenda's engagement ring. He'd chosen it himself and started making payments on layaway, and when he couldn't wait any longer he took his father to the store with him to pay it off. And now there it was—a document attesting to the cut, color, clarity, and carat of a diamond that once upon a time embodied the best of who he was and the grandest of his dreams. He closed his eyes, and as he did his grip relaxed and the document slid out of his hand and down across the slick floor into the pile of trash.

"It's over," he whispered.

Sam stood up and shoved the two piles together and lifted them into a thick black garbage bag. He carried the bag down the side of the apartment building to the dumpster at the end of the parking lot.

The next morning, Sam awoke knowing that the world had changed. He knew he wouldn't be going back to advertising. And the rift between himself and Brenda? He saw now that it had become a canyon, slowly eroded over time. They'd been living together, but not much more than that. Busyness had masqueraded as quality time; conversation had replaced intimacy.

Not sure what to do next, Sam drove across the river and up through East Dallas to White Rock Lake. The lake had once been a place of clarity for him—a place to fill his lungs with clean air, empty his mind of clutter, and let the muse or the spirit or whoever was in control speak to him in its special, mysterious way. He parked at the old boathouse and started walking. The rhythm of the thick muddy water lapping against the shoreline played on his mind and soon he had a plan. Twelve hours later, he was driving south to the coast.

~ ~ ~ ~ ~

"And that's the way it happened," Sam said, his gaze fixed on the water as it had been during the entire saga.

Dave hung his head, wrung out from listening. Out of the corner of his eye he could see Sam's hands clasped tightly as if in prayer, and Dave realized that the last twenty minutes had been nothing short of a full confession. But Dave was no priest, and he had no absolution to give or penance to prescribe. All he had to offer was a silence that he let linger for a while, and then he asked:

"What about the girl . . . Kayla?"

Sam turned and looked Dave in the eye with a piercing stare that made Dave wish not only that he'd not asked that question but that he wasn't sitting next to him now and in fact had never visited Port Aransas. It was not a look of anger. Rather, Dave could see through Sam's dark, dilated pupils down into a bottomless pit of grief. And then he saw Sam blink, and up from that pit flowed the heaviest sobs that Dave had ever heard.

Without the slightest feeling of awkwardness, Dave put his arm around Sam's shoulders and pulled him close. There would be no more questions. He understood the whole of it now: Kayla had died.

After a while the sobs softened and all was quiet again. Sam had torn himself loose from the past, and without saying anything else, he stood up and walked back to his trailer.

Dave lingered for a while and watched the gulls pick at debris that had washed up onto the sand. And then as the light softened and the quiet of dusk descended, Dave walked back to his own room, grateful for the day and hopeful that in time his own liberation would come.

Chapter 16

Shelly was standing over the sink, rinsing out a carafe, and letting her mind wander when the quiet murmur of customers in the room was shattered by the clanging of the door and a loud voice in full conversation. She turned expecting to see two people but there was just one: a short man with thick salt-and-pepper hair, a rumpled suit, a satchel slung over his shoulder, and a cell phone glued to his ear. She watched as he dropped his satchel on top of a table and dug out a laptop computer. She also noticed the irritation on the faces of others in the coffee shop as he continued talking loudly, oblivious to their presence.

"How much credit did we give them? I think a million. I was impressed when we started out . . . young and smart . . . or that's what I thought. Not so sure now. What's that? Yes, I'm here checking things out. Already been to the site. Location here is better, but we have the brand. Gotta go."

The man leaned over, touched a few buttons on his laptop, checked his phone, and then stepped up to the counter.

"I'll take a medium black coffee and something to chew on, no, make that a large coffee and a cinnamon bagel." While Shelly worked on the order, he walked back to the table for a moment, checked his laptop again, then came back. "What's up with your WIFI? I can't get a signal."

"We don't have WIFI," Shelly said.

"Oh . . . really? *Everybody* has WIFI."

"Oh really? And just who is everybody."

"In my case, everybody is Sea Siren."

"Well . . . we don't have WIFI," she said. "That'll be $3.59."

"Well that's at least something, but tell the boss he could charge more for the food if he had WIFI. Gotta have WIFI if you want to be in this game." He handed her a five-dollar bill. "Keep the change, Honey."

Shelly said nothing, but as he walked back to his table, her irritation grew from a low simmer to a boil and finally she couldn't hold back. She opened the register, counted out one dollar and forty-one cents, walked to where the man was sitting, and slapped the change on the table.

"We don't take tips," she said, "and we don't take advice either."

Shelly started to walk back to the counter, but she stopped cold and turned. Her eyes were big, her nostrils flared, but her voice was steady and calm. "I just had that chat with the boss, and I advised myself that we also reserve the right to refuse service, so you can pick up your stuff and get out of here. Now."

He hesitated, not sure what to say, and Shelly made sure he understood.

"Yes, that's right, time for you to go." She pointed at the door. "Now!"

Shocked, he quickly picked up his still-open laptop and placed it in the crook of his left arm, and then with his free hand he put the cell phone in his coat pocket, the bagel in his teeth, the coffee cup in his hand, and he headed toward the door. Just then his phone rang, and without thinking he reached for it, spilling hot coffee on his jacket. The sudden burn in his chest caused him to lose his grip on the bagel, which fell to the floor and rolled across the room, while the laptop slipped off his arm and hit the floor hard.

The noise startled Shelly and she let out a little yip and then a snort of laughter as she saw him trying to pick it all up. He glared at her, and she smirked back at him and said, "Have a nice day."

The room filled with applause from the other customers as Shelly picked up the bagel and threw it in the trash. She smiled as she went back to the counter, but behind her cool look she was terrified. She knew that Sam was right: she was in for a fight.

She was chewing on that thought when she was startled by a "heya" and turned around to find Dave standing at the counter.

"Oh, sorry, I didn't hear you," she said, "otherwise I would have given you a perky coffee shop salute."

"Wow, sounds like you're a little on edge this morning," Dave said. "Anything I can do?"

Shelly sighed and let her frustration bubble out. "Short of passing a law at city hall allowing only local businesses, there's nothing you can do."

Dave's brow wrinkled with questions and Shelly continued, "Sam was right. A man was in here a short while ago and he's obviously in town to find a site for Sea Siren. He was loud and rude and I made him leave."

"Good for you," Dave said. "Sounds like you put him on notice."

"I'm not sure about that since I don't have a plan and don't know what the hell to do," she said.

"Maybe Sam would know," Dave said.

"Oh . . . did you find him? How'd it go?"

"It was . . . let's just say . . . I think he's turned a corner."

"That's good, right?"

"Yes, but . . ."

"But what?"

"He may still be shaky so, like you said yesterday, we shouldn't push him too hard."

"But you said he might know what to do about the shop."

"I think he could help, and it'd be something good for him to work on."

Shelly thought about that for a moment. She was still embarrassed by how she had treated Sam.

"Okay," she said. "I need his help, and it looks like he could use mine. And to make that happen . . . hey, you need to be anywhere else right now?"

"No, I don't have any plans, but I was thinking . . ."

"Great," she said, and she put down the cup towel she'd been twisting and grabbed Dave's hand and pulled him around the edge of the counter. "You know how to run a register?"

"Uh, I'm not really sure I . . ."

"Don't matter. You do know how to count, don't you? I'll just leave the cash drawer open and you can make change. If someone only has a credit card, tell 'em it's on the house."

"Where are you going?" Dave asked.

"I'm going to talk to Sam."

Shelly disappeared into the back and then came back out with her purse and gave Dave a pat on the arm. "I'll be back in an hour. If not, lock the front door and turn off the lights. You can slip out the back. Just pull it shut." And before Dave could object, Shelly was out the door. Dave looked around the room. It was empty, and he hoped it would stay that way till she got back.

Rolling down the highway in her VW Beetle, past the dunes and the trash bins, Shelly's mind traveled back over the past year. She'd lost her family in the accident and might have been a wreck herself had she not thrown all her energy into the Dream Bean. And then Sam had come along and had been a distraction, and not quite a friend but almost, until she pushed him away.

"And what about Dave?" she asked, and then she looked in the rearview mirror to make sure nobody was there because she had surprised herself by saying that out loud. Dave was still a mystery, even more so than Sam, because he seemed to be a loner too but possessed a confidence that Sam lacked or that somehow had been drained out of him. And Dave had a sharp, gentlemanly way that she rather liked and found missing from most of the men on the island that she knew.

Shelly was sorting through those thoughts as she turned onto the road that led down to the trailer park when she suddenly came upon a man walking down the middle of the blacktop. She pressed hard on the brakes and turned the wheel, skidding sideways into the sand.

Furious, she jumped out of the car and launched into him. "Are you freakin' crazy? Are you trying to get yourself killed? What the hell are you doing walking down the middle of the . . ." but she didn't finish the sentence because as the dust cleared she saw that it was Sam and he was holding up his hands as if to surrender to an enemy.

Shelly caught her breath and lowered her voice. "Oh Sam, I'm so sorry . . . it's just . . . I came so close to running you down . . . it frightened me."

She took another deep breath and watched as he

lowered his arms with a look of not knowing whether to continue walking or turn and go home.

"So, where are you going?" Shelly asked.

"I was going to the market to apologize to Ms. Gifford for leaving and to see if I can get my job back," he said.

"Well that's a good thing," Shelly said.

"And then I was going to apologize to you."

"To me? For what?"

"For running away. I've been running away too long. I can't fix the past, but I can do something about the present, and I want to tell you I'm sorry."

"But I ran you off. I told you to leave."

"You had good reason. I put my nose in your business where it didn't belong."

"And I was stubborn," she said. "I didn't want to face the truth. And you know, you were right. A man came in the shop this morning and he left no doubt he's with Sea Siren and he's looking for a site."

"Hmm," Sam said.

"And then of course I ran him off too," Shelly said. "That's what I do."

That brought a smile to Sam's face, one of the few that Shelly had ever seen on him. She smiled back. "So, can I give you a lift to the market?"

"No, that's okay, I like to walk. It'll give me time to plan what I want to say."

"You'll do fine," Shelly said, "but don't give all your time back to Maggie. I really do need your help now."

Chapter 17

Dave looked at his watch and when he was certain that an hour had passed, he walked to the front door, locked it, flipped the Open sign to Closed, and turned off the lights. He did as Shelly directed and walked out the back alley door and pulled it shut. He was jiggling the knob to make sure it was locked when a hand grabbed the back of his shirt collar and shoved him against the wall.

"Hey wait . . ."

But before Dave could say more his arm was bent behind his back and the leverage forced him face-first into the ground.

"Wait a minute . . ." he tried again, but he was cut off by a burly voice.

"I'll teach you to mess with sister. What are you doing skulking around here? Tell me or you'll be eatin' gravel."

"Shelly asked me to look after the shop."

"Liar. Shelly wouldn't do that. She don't let nobody help her. What'd you take?" and he started going through Dave's pockets.

"I was locking up. I didn't take anything."

"Don't lie to me, son."

"Come on, I don't have anything. The store is locked."

Dave felt his attacker release one hand, and he braced for a blow when another voice broke in.

"Get off him, Bo."

Dave turned his head toward the voice and saw Shelly running toward them.

"Let him go, now," she shouted.

Dave felt the weight ease off his back, and he rolled over and looked up to see the balding old fisherman in the stained coveralls.

Shelly knelt beside Dave. "Are you okay?"

"Sure," he said, sitting up and brushing the sand and grit off his face. Shelly reached up and gently turned his head from side to side to see for herself. Convinced, she stood up and turned to Bo.

"Dang it, Bo, what were you thinking?"

"I was thinking that this man was breaking into your shop."

"This man was doing exactly what I asked him to do. He was locking up for me. And now you owe him an apology."

"For what? I just did what anybody else would have done if they'd seen a stranger rattling around your back door."

Dave, still sitting on the ground between them, listened with interest as Shelly handled this man twice her age and twice her size.

"In addition to him doing what I told him, this man is no stranger. He has a name, and his name is Dave, and so you owe Dave an apology."

"How was I supposed to know any of that? I've never seen this man before."

"Well, you should have asked him before you started beating on him."

"I didn't beat on him," Bo said. "I just . . . sat on him a little."

"Well you were wrong and you owe . . ."

"It's okay," Dave said as he stood up. "I'm not hurt. He didn't know who I was."

"Oh, so that's the way it is, you're siding with him now?" Shelly said, focusing her irritation on Dave. "You men always gang up when a woman is in the room."

Dave and Bo watched as Shelly walked away to the corner of the building and said, "Come on," as she turned out of sight. They looked at each other and then followed her up the steps and into the Dream Bean.

Shelly went behind the counter and started brewing a pot of coffee. She pointed to a table, which Dave and Bo understood was where they were being told to sit. Following her directions, they sat across from each other, silently waiting to see what would happen next. Dave cast a sideways glance at Bo, and Bo did the same, though they both pretended not to notice. Shelly came to the table with a tray loaded with four mugs, a pot of coffee, and a plate of cookies. She sat down and poured a cup for each of them and herself.

"Well?" she questioned, took a sip, put her mug down, and turned to Bo. "Have you apologized yet?"

"No, you heard him. He said that wasn't necessary."

"I don't care what Dave said. I still want you to apologize."

"This is one tough sister," Bo said as if to warn Dave, and then like the gentleman that he wasn't, he stood up and extended his hand. "I apologize, sir."

"Accepted," Dave said as he shook Bo's large weathered hand.

"Much better." Shelly relaxed her expression and allowed a slight smile to cross her face.

Just at that moment, as if on cue, Sam came in the door. He hesitated when he saw the three of them at the table, but Shelly motioned to him and he quietly walked over and sat in the one empty chair. Shelly filled the fourth mug and placed it in front of Sam.

"Okay, we're all here," she said. "Let's get started."

Shelly retold what she had heard from her obnoxious customer that morning, and Sam went over the conversation he heard a week earlier at the bank.

"It definitely sounds like something is up, but maybe we should make sure," said Dave. "I could go to the bank and pose as a new business owner needing a loan. I could say something like, 'How's the business climate around here? Anybody new coming to town?'"

This was all news to Bo who listened as he gulped his

coffee. He didn't care for outsiders, and Dave fit into that group, but the idea of corporate types coming to town and pushing people around set him off even more.

"Want me to help you run 'em off?" he said. "I can take 'em out in my boat and sort of lose 'em out there."

"Don't be stupid," Shelly said. "We're not going to hurt anyone."

"Well then, what can I do?"

"Advertising," Sam said.

"Huh?" Bo asked.

"Sure, he can talk up the shop around town," Shelly said.

"It's more subtle than that," Sam said. "We can use his image."

Shelly looked at Bo and then Sam. "I don't know about that. I mean, no offense, but . . ."

"What do you have in mind?" Dave interjected.

"One of the things that made Sea Siren popular is they have an image, a visual. It's that sea lion on every sign and cup. Dream Bean is a great name, but there's no mental picture that goes with that."

"Have you really looked at this man?" Shelly said, gesturing toward Bo.

"Now wait just a minute, sister," Bo said.

"Hold on you two," Dave said. "He's not talking about an actual image; he's talking about a perception."

"More like a myth," Sam said. "The myth and mystery of the sea. Shelly is the pretty harbor maiden, and Bo is the solid, steady sailor she conjures when she drinks that perfect cup of coffee."

"Pretty harbor maiden? Ha," Bo said loudly. "That's a myth for sure."

"Neither of you are the real characters," Sam said, "but it helps that there's a real Shelly. And, it doesn't hurt that she has friends who are sailors. It ties the shop to a real time and place. It provides the basis for a fictional narrative."

"Wow, you've really been thinking about this," Shelly said. "Dave said you were good, but I'm really impressed."

Sam looked down at the table, embarrassed.

"Well done, Sam. What happens next?" Dave asked, tapping Shelly's foot with his toe to make note of Sam's discomfort. Shelly caught the signal and followed along.

"Oh, yeah, well . . . maybe we all need to let that sink in and get back together in a day or two. It's getting late anyway. How about just after closing time tomorrow?"

Everyone agreed, and they stood up from the table. Bo and Sam both walked toward the door. Bo walked on out into the growing darkness while Sam hesitated a moment.

"Do you need a ride home?" Dave asked.

"No, I'll be okay," he said. "I was just thinking . . . what if I'm wrong about all of this?"

"Then we're all wrong together because we're gonna do this together," Shelly said. "By the way, how'd it go with Maggie at the market?"

"She said she can work me back into the schedule starting next week."

"Great," Shelly said, "but like I said earlier, save some time to work on our project here. We'll figure out what that means later."

Sam nodded and walked out the door.

When it was clear that Sam and Bo were both out of sight, Shelly spoke. "Well . . . that was interesting."

"Yes, it was," Dave said. "I wasn't expecting Sam to come on so strong, but then he retreated just as fast. Like we said, we need to go easy on him."

There was a long pause as both stood with the table between them. Dave's mind was spinning. He wanted to linger but he wasn't sure why, or what he would do if he did. He realized the pause was becoming awkward and finally said, "Okay, I'll see you tomorrow."

That night, each one, in their own way, laid out their hopes and dreams, their sorrows and losses, their successes and failures, and wondered what the new day would bring.

Sam walked alone back to the trailer, this time walking down the beach instead of the highway. He felt like he was learning to walk again and he wasn't sure if he could keep himself upright. He worried that if he fell, the others would tumble with him.

Dave drove back to his hotel and didn't even notice that he hadn't passed Sam along the way. His thoughts were cloudy, his heart riding a pendulum between the old life that had died and a new life still being born.

Shelly locked up the shop and drove silently back to her house. She knew she had bulled and bullied her way through her grief and the effort had created her business. She liked her independence, but she knew she needed help now.

Bo walked down the pier to his boat and sat down on the cot in the little compartment at the back of the pilothouse. He looked around at what for twenty years had been his home. He recalled how it had felt like a cell the first night he slept there, so different from where he had come, but now it felt like home. He worried that all this attention they talked about would complicate things. Worse, it would expose him.

Chapter 18

Bo pulled the throttle back and eased the *Cassie* out of the marina. Looking over his shoulder, he saw the lights from the Dream Bean glowing through the early morning fog and knew Shelly was inside getting ready for the day. He wished he could be there to help her fight to keep the shop going, but she'd have to go on without him. Right now, he had some business of his own to clear up.

Turning north, he pushed up the coast and several hours later came to Surfside Beach. He turned the bow toward the port side and let the channel absorb the *Cassie* back into the inland waterways. He floated up past the Coast Guard station to the point of Brazosport and on around the channel beyond the refineries to Freeport and into an empty slip. When he had everything squared away, he stepped onto the dock and began walking down the familiar streets to the little white wood frame house that once was home. Standing at the curb, he looked it over. The shrubs had grown up over the top of the porch railing, and the stained glass above the door that had once glowed warmly was shuttered over.

He was noticing how the lace curtains had been replaced with mini blinds when he saw movement in the window and then heard the latch on the front door release. Bo stepped backward off the curb as the door opened and a young woman stepped onto the porch.

"Something I can do for you, mister?"

Bo paused a moment. "I'm looking for someone . . . someone who lived here a long time ago."

"Don't know if I can help. We've been here just a few years. We came with DuPont."

"Oh, I see," said Bo. "You don't know anything about who was here previously, do you?"

"No, we're just renting. Maybe it's our landlord you're looking for. He lives over in Texas City."

"No, I was looking for . . . a woman . . . she owned the house. Sorry to bother you."

"That's okay," she said, and went back inside.

Disappointed, and a little relieved too, Bo began walking back through town. But the more he walked, the more irritated with himself he became until he was practically in a froth. It was while in that mood that he spied the police station down on a corner and went bursting through the front door and to the desk.

"I want to turn myself in," he said to the sergeant sitting at the front desk.

"Oh you do, huh? And just what is it you've done that you need to get turned in for?"

"Negligence."

The sergeant thought about that a moment, looking over the grizzled man in front of him and discerning from his attire that he was a fisherman.

"Well, skipper, you're gonna have to be more specific than that. There's all kinds of negligence, and while a lot of it's stupid, not all of it's criminal."

Bo was quiet for a moment. He'd floated all the way from Port Aransas with words in his head, but now he had to say them out loud. He swallowed, and then spoke plainly. "I fathered a child, but then I left the mother high and dry and now I want to own up to it."

"Hmm . . . ." The sergeant looked at Bo, thought for a moment, and then began tapping the keys on his computer. "I know fatherhood knows no age limits, and we might have an abandonment claim here on file. When did this happen . . . give me the month first."

"It was twenty years ago. I don't reckon I recall the month," Bo said.

The sergeant took his hands off the keyboard and looked up at Bo. "Now look here, skipper, I don't have time or the patience for horsing around. We've got real people with real problems, and this sounds to me like a family issue. Unless you've physically hurt someone or stolen their property, and unless you've done it within the past two years, you're in the wrong place."

Bo shifted in his boots and after a moment he tried a different tack. "Then how about helping me find a missing person?"

"And just who would that be . . . and don't tell me that it's you."

Bo leaned forward, cleared his throat, and in a hushed voice spoke aloud the name that he had been holding inside for twenty years: "Cassandra Dupree."

"Doesn't ring a bell, but I'll take a look here." As the sergeant began typing into his computer again, Bo heard boots scuffing on the floor and looked up to see an older uniformed man coming from the next room. The nameplate above his shirt pocket flap said "Ragan," and etched into his silver shield was the word "Chief."

"Just who are you?" Ragan asked.

"Bo . . . er . . . ," and he straightened his shoulders and raised his head, "Beauregard Savoy."

"And you're looking for Cassandra Dupree?"

"Yes. You know her?"

Chief Ragan put his hand on the sergeant's shoulder. "I'll handle this, Bobby. You go get some lunch."

"Sure thing, Chief," the sergeant said, obeying, but hesitant because he was curious to know what these two older men were going to talk about. Ragan watched silently as the young sergeant got his cap and keys and walked out the front door, and then he turned his attention back to Bo and motioned for him to sit down.

"Now, what's your relationship to Cassandra?"

"I was her husband . . . common law husband, that is. I was hoping to see her . . . make amends . . . or at least apologize."

The chief leaned back in his chair and rubbed his chin a moment. "I'm sorry sir . . . Mr. Savoy . . . but that won't be possible."

"Why not?"

"She's not here."

"So you know her? Where is she?"

Ragan paused to form the next sentence. "We don't know. Nobody's seen her since Hurricane Ike. Best we can tell she was out in the storm and got swept away."

There was a long silence, and Ragan watched quietly as Bo's eyes turned wet. Finally, Bo asked, "And her daughter?"

"You mean, your daughter, don't you?" He stared into Bo's face. No words came from Bo's mouth, but his eyes said everything.

"She's okay," Ragan continued. "All grown up. Lives here in town."

"What's her name? Where can I find her?"

"Her name is Allie, and I wouldn't go bother her if I were you. Bad enough that her mother is missing. Having her father suddenly turn up might be more shock than she can take."

"Sure, I understand," Bo said quietly. "Still, is there some way I can see . . ."

"She works at Walmart," Ragan interrupted.

"Thanks." Bo stood to shake the chief's hand.

A few minutes later, Bo was standing inside Walmart, his eyes drawn to everyone he saw who was wearing a blue vest. Nobody looked familiar, although he really didn't know who he was looking for, and he was beginning to think this was a bad idea when from behind him he heard a soft lilting voice ask, "Can I help you sir?" Bo turned around and looked directly into the face of a young girl who was the mirror image of the woman he once loved. As he stared into the bright blue eyes that he remembered from long ago, he felt a tightness in his chest and then his head became as heavy as a cinder block.

"Sir?" the girl asked, and that was the last thing Bo heard.

~ ~ ~ ~ ~

Two hours later, Shelly was at the Dream Bean getting ready for the evening meeting. Dave and Sam were walking in the door when the phone rang. Shelly answered, and then she listened, responding only with "yes" and after a long pause, "OK." She put the phone down and switched off the coffee maker.

"What's up?" Dave asked.

"It's Bo," Shelly said as she grabbed her purse and walked briskly toward the door. "I'll tell you on the way."

"On the way? Where are we going?" Dave asked.

"Freeport."

Chapter 19

"Well, Bo, what'd you get yourself into this time?" Shelly asked as she made a quick scan of the monitors on the wall next to the hospital bed. Her slim knowledge of blood pressures and pulse rates told her that Bo was in no danger.

"This time? Whadaya mean by that? There's never been no other time," Bo said.

"Well most folks don't just fall over in the middle of Walmart. Speaking of which, what were you doing at Walmart in Freeport, of all crazy things?"

"Just needed some supplies, that's all."

"Well, honey, we have stores closer to home. We can go for you if you need something. Why, Sam is at the market every day."

"Is he here, too?" Bo craned his head to look out into the hallway.

"Yes, and Dave."

"You didn't have to bring the whole damn town." Bo turned to hide his embarrassment.

"Don't be worrying about that." Shelly patted him on the shoulder. "I asked them to come along so we could figure out how to get you back home."

Shelly looked out into the hallway and saw Dave talking to a young girl wearing a blue vest.

"Who's that?" Shelly asked.

"Oh, just some girl that was near me when I fell," said Bo. "You can tell her to go back to work now that you're here."

"Well it was nice of her to come check on you," Shelly said.

As she spoke a doctor came in. "Feeling better, Mr. Savoy?"

"Yep. Ready to go."

"And is this your family?"

"Close as I've got."

"Yes, we're all he's got," said Shelly, pointing to Dave and Sam in the hallway.

"Well then I can tell you that the pictures and blood samples we took show no indications of cardiac or neurological issues. I suspect what Mr. Savoy had was just a common fainting spell. Didn't help that he hadn't eaten in twelve hours. So . . . we're going to keep him overnight, keep him on an IV, get some real food in him, and let him get some rest. You can take him home in the morning."

"Morning? I'm ready to go now," Bo said. "I can sleep on the boat tonight and turn her back home in the morning."

"No way," Shelly interrupted. "You're gonna do just

what the doctor said, and we'll worry about the boat tomorrow."

"Perfect," said the doctor. "I'll see you all in the morning. Goodnight."

When the doctor was gone, Dave came in. "Okay, I think we've got a plan." And then he laid it all out: Dave would drive back to Port Aransas with Shelly so she could get back to the Dream Bean in the morning. Sam would stay in Freeport and sleep in the guest room at the Walmart girl's house, at her invitation. "Her name is Allie, by the way," Dave said. Allie would drive Sam and Bo back to the boat in the morning. And Sam would float back down the coast with Bo.

"Sam, that beach bum?" Bo said while Sam was still in the hall.

"Yes, he crewed with a shrimper for a while so he'll make a better mate than any of the rest of us," Dave said.

At that moment, Sam and Allie came in the room and she walked around the end of the bed to give Bo a pat on the shoulder. "You get some rest, Mr. Savoy," and as she turned to leave, Shelly, Dave, and Sam all saw the same thing: Allie and Bo shared the same slight curl of the lip and crinkle at the top of the nose.

On the drive back to Port Aransas, Shelly was the first to talk about it. "It's got to be a coincidence."

"Maybe so," Dave said, "but on the other hand, what do you really know about Bo? And who is *Cassie* who his boat is named for? And what was he doing in Freeport? You saw how much they look alike."

"Yes, but Bo said she was just the girl who was standing there when he fainted. It could have been anyone standing there."

"But maybe he went there to see her," said Dave.

"But in the hospital they acted like total strangers."

"Maybe they . . . maybe she . . ."

"Maybe what?"

"Oh, nothing," said Dave.

They continued up the highway in silence, but both were still trying to figure it out.

Back in Freeport, Allie gathered bed linens from a closet and led Sam to her small but neat guest room.

"Here ya go. It's not much, but it's clean," she said.

"It's plenty," Sam said. "So . . . are you always this open to total strangers?"

"My mother was always helping others. Didn't matter how well she knew them. She just trusted the goodness in everyone. Anyway . . . just shout if you need anything else. Otherwise, I'll see you in the morning." Allie left the room and disappeared down the hall.

Sam made up the bed—which he realized was the first real bed he had slept in since leaving Dallas—and then he stripped down to his underwear and crawled between the sheets. Not only had he forgotten what a real bed felt like, but the cool, soapy smell of the sheets made him realize that he couldn't remember the last time he'd washed the ragged sheets back in the trailer. His obsessive drive for order had been another casualty of his flight from his previous lifestyle. As he drifted off to sleep, he promised himself to get that back some day.

Down the coast, Shelly cut her speed and let Dave point out the dark entrance to the hotel parking lot. They rolled up the drive and Dave directed her to the side of the building and the outside stairs. "I'm up here."

Shelly pulled into an empty parking space, idled for a moment, and then cut the engine. The windows were down and the cool air passing across the front seat caused her to lean back in her seat and close her eyes.

"What are you thinking about?" Dave asked.

"Nothing."

"Really? Nothing?"

"Just enjoying the breeze. I'm not out late very often. I forget how nice it can be after the sun sets and the breeze comes in."

"You don't hang out with friends or whatever?"

"No, not with friends . . . or whatever."

"Hmm . . ."

"Hmm what?"

"It's just . . . I figured a girl like you has a pretty active social life."

"I have to be at the shop early. Doesn't leave time for much else."

"Thought about getting some help?"

"Thought about it, but can't afford it."

"Not even part time?"

Shelly let out a long sigh. "Not even."

"You're going to need some help if you're going to fight off Sea Siren."

Shelly turned in her seat to face Dave. "And what about that? Do you really think I have a chance?"

"I don't know if *you* have a chance, but *we* do . . . all of us, together."

Shelly settled back into her seat, looking straight ahead out the windshield, her right hand resting on top of the stick shift. Dave reached over to give her hand a reassuring pat, but then his hand lingered and he let his fingers fall between hers. Shelly moved her thumb ever so slightly, letting it rub against Dave's little finger, and then she lifted her hand and Dave withdrew.

"Well . . ."

"It's getting late," he said.

"Yes."

"What time do you think they'll get in tomorrow?" Dave asked.

"Don't know, but I'll call you if I see or hear anything. What's your room number?"

"205." Dave pulled the latch and pushed open the door, then he turned to look at Shelly again.

"What?" she asked.

He paused, wanting to say something, but nothing came out except, "Goodnight."

Dave watched as Shelly drove away and then climbed

up the stairs but stopped and sat down on the top step, looking out toward the shimmer of the Gulf in the moonlight. He couldn't hear the breakers over the pounding of his pulse in his ears. He knew that something had just happened, maybe something very small, but it frightened and excited him all at once.

Driving home, Shelly felt it too, and she wasn't sure if she was ready for it or even wanted it. Most of all, she was afraid she couldn't stop it if she tried.

Chapter 20

Awakening to the smell of bacon, Sam dressed, stopped in the hall bathroom to wash his face and comb his hair with his hands, then made his way to the kitchen where Allie was working at the stove.

"That looks good. Is there something I can do to help?" he asked.

"Nope, I'm almost done here."

Sam sat down at the table that Allie had already set. Watching her face as she worked—that face that he, Shelly, and Dave had all seemed to recognize at the hospital—he started to probe a little.

"So how long have you known Bo, that is, Mr. Savoy?"

"I don't know him at all."

"Have you seen him in the store before?"

"No. We get enough regulars that I know some by face, but we also get vacationers and newcomers, so it's not unusual to see strangers."

"Did he say what he was shopping for?"

"No, he never said anything. I asked if he needed anything and when he turned around he looked at me and hit the floor. What's this about? Is he a fugitive or something?" she laughed.

"No, it's just . . . well, we all thought we knew him, but it turns out we don't really know him at all."

"Isn't that the way it is with most of us? We have lots of acquaintances but not too many friends—at least not the type who share much?"

Sam didn't answer, but he knew it was true. He'd managed to spend more than a year in Port Aransas without really getting to know anyone at all.

"Do you have family around?" Sam asked.

"No, just here by myself."

"And your parents . . . in another town?"

"They're dead." She walked to the table with the frying pan and nudged some eggs and bacon onto both of their plates before setting the pan back on the stove and sitting down across from Sam. She bowed her head for a moment then crossed herself, looked up at Sam, and blushed. "Let's eat."

Sam was taken by her no-nonsense, get-down-to-business way of doing things. She was like Bo, only more gentle.

After breakfast, Sam helped Allie clean up—as much as she would allow, which was only to dry the dishes after she washed them—and then they got in her little Toyota and drove the mile to the hospital. When they got to Bo's room, he was already dressed and looking out the window.

"You're late," Bo frowned.

"Late? We never specified a time," Sam said.

"The minute the sun came up you were late. Let's go."

"Wait a minute, shouldn't you wait for the doctor?" Allie asked.

"Already been here. Wasn't late like you." Bo waved a folded set of papers in his hand.

"Oh, but aren't they supposed to . . . ." Before Allie could finish, Bo was walking past her and out the door. Allie and Sam caught up with Bo in the hallway and walked with him out the door and out to the car. Sam climbed into the back seat so Bo could direct Allie to the pier where the boat was docked.

Bo jumped out of the front seat before Allie put the car into park and began walking ahead, calling over his shoulder to Sam. "If you'll give me a hand with the lines, we'll be ready to go."

"What time do you have to be at work?" Sam asked Allie.

"I'm off today."

"Then come with us."

Bo stopped walking and wheeled around. "Now wait a minute. I don't think that's such a good idea. It may be a rough trip with the wind kicking up like it is, and this old boat could break down, and well . . ."

"Nonsense," Sam said. "The weather's fine today. Besides, we could probably use an extra pair of hands."

"Are you sure?" Allie asked.

"No, dammit, he's not sure at all. This ain't his boat and he has no right to be making invitations." Bo turned red from the crown of his bald head to his chin as he shouted at them both.

"I promise I won't be in the way, Mr. Savoy," Allie said. "I'll just sit quietly, or if you need me to do something, then just say so and I'll do it."

"See," said Sam. "I really do think it will be fine."

Bo glared at Sam and then turned and spit into the water as he hopped onto the deck. "You just don't understand."

"What?" Sam asked.

There was a long pause, and realizing he'd talked himself to the edge of disclosure, Bo pointed a big meaty finger at both Sam and Allie. "You just mind what I say and maybe this'll turn out okay."

And as soon as he said that he seemed to shrink within himself, and Sam and Allie both jumped to his side and helped him sit down on top of the tool box on the forward deck.

"Are you sure *you* should be making this trip?" Allie asked, searching Sam's eyes for any hint of agreement or doubt.

"I'm fine," Bo said in a whispery voice. "Laying in the hospital drained my energy. Just need to get on back to where I belong."

So with Bo giving orders, Sam and Allie got a few

loose items stowed away and untied the boat from its moorings. Then, with Bo and Allie sitting on the deck, Sam went into the pilothouse, turned the engine on, and slowly moved the throttle back.

"Easy . . . easy . . . gotta be patient . . . she'll come along when she's ready," Bo said as the gears engaged and the boat backed into the channel. "Neutral now . . . let her drift . . . that's right." Bo stood up and checked either side, and once the boat had cleared the end of the dock and the other boats, he shouted, "Okay, forward now . . . gradual . . . that's right."

With Bo continuing to give orders, they made their way past the refineries and the Coast Guard station and then Sam pointed the bow out into the open water.

As they churned along in the morning sunshine, Allie noticed how Bo's eyes darted nervously from the bow to Sam and back again.

"Seems like he's doing a good job," Allie said.

Bo didn't answer. In all his anxiety of having newcomers aboard and getting the boat fit for travel and on its way, he'd let go of his worries that this young girl sitting right next to him was probably his flesh-and-blood daughter. Now that thought was foremost in his mind, and he was afraid to speak to her.

"Steady as she goes there Sam," he said, choosing to stick to his immediate role as captain.

"Aye aye," said Sam in his best old sailor voice. From where he was standing at the wheel he could see Bo and

Allie in profile, and the resemblance was striking. It was evident not just in their faces but in their posture. There was even something in their voices—perhaps a touch of Cajun dialect—that seemed to connect them in a way that couldn't be a coincidence.

As Allie's long hair tossed and tangled in the Gulf wind, Sam remembered how Kayla's hair had bounced in the breeze on that midnight when she climbed into his car for the drive that would end her young life. Seeing Allie and Bo sitting together, Sam realized for the first time that his carelessness had stolen Kayla away from her father. He closed his eyes in shame for a moment because in the chaos of that time he had never reached out to Kayla's family—not to sit with them at the hospital; not to offer an apology, lame as it might have been; not to offer condolences some weeks later when injuries that seemed superficial at first took her young life. He realized too that he had built a life in which he was the center of all his attention, with no time for a loving relationship, no time for children, and no time to even understand what it was like to have the love of a daughter stolen in a moment of carelessness. When Sam opened his eyes again and looked out at the old sailor sitting on the deck with his daughter, he decided that he wasn't going to let Bo be so proud and scared not to claim the daughter that he had.

At that precise instant Bo glanced at the pilothouse and caught Sam's piercing stare. He turned back toward the Gulf but he couldn't escape Sam's voice.

"Hey, Bo, need some help in here a moment."

"What is it now," Bo huffed, trying to mask his fear with his usual irritation. He stood, making sure he had his balance, before walking back into the pilothouse. "What is it?"

Sam whispered: "I was just wondering—when are you going to tell her?"

"What the hell are you talking about?" Bo said loudly.

"You know what I'm talking about. It's obvious to us, and she's going to see it too if she's around you long enough."

"And that's why I told you she shouldn't come, but you wouldn't listen to me. You just mind your own business, and while you're at it, get the hell away from my boat." And he pushed Sam away from the controls and pointed toward the door.

Allie was completely oblivious to the fact that these two men were arguing about her just a few feet away. With her face turned toward the sunshine, she let herself bask in the warmth of the morning and the peaceful rhythm of the motor and sporadic thud of the bow bucking against the waves.

They made the rest of the trip mostly in silence, with Sam and Allie making occasional small talk while Bo brooded inside. After an hour, Sam began to see familiar landmarks on the shore—the private developments, the hotels, and the long stretch of beach that led to the trailer park. It felt good to be coming back to what had become his home.

Bo maneuvered the boat past the jetty and to the pier, and then he cut the engine and let the boat drift to the piece of dock that had been his for years.

"Okay you two, let's tie her down." Bo tossed a line off the bow and another off the stern. Sam and Allie scrambled off the deck, with Sam securing the bow and Allie kneeling down to tie off at the stern.

"She's a good boat," Allie said, and then she stood up and for the first time saw the name *Cassie* painted in faded green letters across the back.

Chapter 21

Allie sat down on a piling and tried to get her thoughts straight. She'd never known her father and when she asked about him her mother just brushed it off in a casual way: "He was just a guy I knew once, just a fling, no big deal." Allie heard some mention of a "fisherman" a few times when her mother was talking to girlfriends, but without a name or sense of emotion in the reference, Allie didn't dig any deeper.

But now as she looked across the boat at this gruff, grizzled, bald-headed man with her mother's name painted across the stern of his boat, it was starting to make sense—why he was standing in Walmart in a town where he didn't live, and why he dropped to the floor as soon as he turned and saw her. It wasn't such an odd reaction after all, and had she known who he was, she might have fainted too. After all, that's what she felt like doing now.

Seeing Allie sitting in a state of bewilderment, Sam sat down beside her. As Bo clanked around on the boat behind them, Sam asked, "You okay?"

"I'm not sure," she said. "Is it true?"

"Maybe. Can't say for sure."

"Why now?"

"You'll have to ask him. It's like I said this morning: We thought we knew Bo, but it turns out we don't."

After another pause that might have been soothing if it wasn't for Bo making a racket on the boat, Allie spoke again: "So, what do I do now?"

"Only you can decide that. But I suspect the two of you need to talk, and you need to do that in private."

Sam stood up and pointed to the green awning with the words "Shelly's Dream Bean" that could be seen beyond the forest of boat masts. "I'll be just over there. You come on over whenever you want to. We'll make sure you get a ride back to Freeport."

Allie watched Sam walk away and for a moment she forgot about Bo, intrigued by this other quiet, gentle man. Why couldn't he be my father, she thought, and then she shook her head at how ridiculous that was. She didn't even really want or need a father, and now that she apparently had one, she wasn't sure what she was supposed to do with him.

When Bo turned from his work and saw Allie sitting alone, he had the same thoughts: What do I do now? He had nothing to offer this girl that would in any way make amends for abandoning her and Cassandra so many years ago. He shook his head at the absurdity of how he'd gone in search of her when he had no plan or consideration of the consequences.

Bo sat down on the toolbox with a loud groan. Allie turned quickly, thinking Bo might be in trouble again, and for the longest moment father and daughter just stared at each other from twenty feet away. She blinked and he blinked. She brushed a stray hair off of her face, and he coughed a little, but their eyes remained locked until Allie broke the trance.

"Why did you bring me here?"

Bo shrugged, not quite understanding the question.

"Why am I here? What is this about?" As she spoke she stood up and began walking toward him, the questions coming one after another, not waiting for an answer. "Who are you? Why did you come looking for me? What did you expect to find?" and when she was right on top of him, "What do you want from me?"

Allie stared down at him, her nostrils flaring.

Bo's eyes watered a little. "God, you look just like her."

Allie sat down beside him, exactly where she had been sitting as they churned down the coast from Freeport, but now with a knowledge of him that she didn't have earlier and emotions that felt strange and foreign.

"Well?" she asked again, "what is this about?"

Bo looked down at his leathery hands, the only part of his entire being that really held the answers to her questions. Hands that had gripped tools and worked on motors, pulled in nets and been sliced up by shells and broken glass. Hands that had smelled of fish and oil and cheap cologne. Hands that had once held a woman so gently, and then one night had unlatched a gate and carried a duffle bag into the darkness.

"I don't know," he finally said. "I just wanted to see her one more time, to see if maybe she'd had a good life, a life I couldn't give her."

Allie now found herself in the odd position of having to speak for someone else, but as she thought about that she smiled because she knew what her mother would want her to say.

"She had a good life, but it wasn't because you left her. She knows—I know—that you meant well, but she didn't need anything different from you or from anyone else to make her life good. She had a good life because that's who she was."

Bo nodded. "She was good. There's no doubting that. And that's . . ." Bo hung his head for a moment, rubbing his dirty hands together as if that would change things.

"And that's what?" Allie asked.

"That's why I left. I thought as sweet and kind as she was, she could do better with someone else."

There was silence for a moment. Bo straightened up and looked around, noticing that the pier was unusually quiet. "What day is it?"

"Sunday," Allie answered.

"Oh, that explains why there's nobody around. Your mother always went to church on Sundays. I'd sleep in, but she'd get up and go. Said it helped everything make sense to her. I never really understood that."

"She never gave me that choice," Allie said. "She'd take me kicking and screaming sometimes, but she said I was too young to decide for myself. When I got older, she let me do what I wanted."

"What'd ya do?"

"I went with her. She was the light of my life." Allie tossed her hair back, letting the sun bathe her face.

"Where was she going when the storm hit?" Bo asked.

"She was taking groceries to a lady from the church who couldn't get out. I tried to talk her out of it but she wouldn't listen. She said we needed ice cream anyway."

Bo chuckled.

"What?" Allie asked.

"She was strong-willed . . . and she always had to have her ice cream. I'm glad that didn't change."

"Yes, but it likely killed her." Allie stood up and brushed off her pants.

"Maybe so, but she was just being who she was, and she wasn't afraid of nothing."

"And what were you afraid of, Mr. Savoy? Or should I call you Dad?"

Bo stood up too and fumbled for his pockets. "Everything," he said.

"That doesn't tell me anything."

"Providing for her, being steady . . . and that, what you just called me . . . I just didn't think I could be who she wanted me to be, or what you both would need.

I mean . . . look at me." He stretched his arms out as if to enlarge his deficiencies.

"Honestly, did she ever ask you to be someone or something other than who you were?"

"Well no, but . . ." He stopped. There was no explaining what even he didn't understand.

"So . . . Bo . . . that's what I'll call you for now . . . what do we do?"

"I guess we work on getting you home."

~ ~ ~ ~ ~

At the Dream Bean, Shelly, Sam, and Dave were sitting at a table, making small talk about what might be happening just a short distance away when the door opened and Bo and Allie walked in. They all stood as if on cue and waited for some indication of what to do next.

"We need to get this girl home," Bo said.

"I don't want to go home, not just yet anyway." Allie crossed her arms. She'd made her decision on the short walk over. The others all looked at each other.

"Well, you can't stay with me. You've seen I got no room on the boat," Bo said.

"I've just got the trailer," Sam piped in.

"And I'm in a hotel room . . . which I need to vacate tomorrow and get back to Dallas," Dave said.

They all looked at Shelly, but Allie interjected. "I'm not asking for anything from any of you." Everyone relaxed their posture a little. "I came here because I wanted to and I can get a motel room."

There was a brief silence, and then Shelly spoke. "Nonsense. I have a spare room. You can have it as long as you like."

"Well, then, that seems to be settled," said Dave.

Chapter 22

After the intrigue of the trip to Freeport, Sam was content to go back to work at the market where things were mundane by comparison. The doings with Bo and Allie had brought Sam further out into the light, and he was ready to retreat into the shadows. The market was the perfect place for that. Sam was still a stranger to most of the customers, and the work kept him busy with little conversation.

The anonymity he enjoyed in that setting also gave him the chance to mull over the storm that was brewing in his head over who he had been in the past, who he was now, and who he was to be in the future. He'd grown to like the quiet, contemplative man who wandered the beach at sunrise and sunset and hid out in the trailer during the day. He liked the freedom of doing whatever he pleased, which often was nothing at all. On the other hand, he was starting to enjoy the little bursts of adrenaline that he got from talking business with Shelly and Dave. But that scared him because he had let that get out of hand in Dallas. He didn't ever want to be that man again.

Those thoughts were on Sam's mind early the next morning as he took his regular walk on the beach. More than anything, he had a new feeling of contentment and an understanding that the time had come to quit worrying about the failings of the past and begin claiming the life that was happening right here and now. This is all there is. There is no more yesterday, and there is no tomorrow. There is only now. And so, Sam made a quiet vow to himself to live in that present place. Rehabilitation or a return to something was not the goal. The goal was simply to live.

With that feeling in his heart Sam started up the highway to the Dream Bean. He had no agenda for what he would do when he got there, because to have an agenda, one has to have a preconception of what the conditions will be. He didn't know and he didn't care. He'd walk in and what he found would dictate who he was and what he would be. In that way, he'd be a true man of the world, one in being with the world. He was ceding control to the world—or perhaps to creation or to God, if that really was at the core of everything that was.

With that high-minded manifesto in his soul, Sam entered the Dream Bean and found Shelly behind the counter, working with pad and pencil, while Allie was wiping down the condiment table. Allie looked up and when she saw Sam her face lit up with a big smile.

"Good morning, Sam," she said.

"Good morning to you, Allie . . . and you too, Shelly."

"Uh huh," Shelly said, acknowledging Sam but not looking up. "Be with you in a moment."

"I'll take care of him." Allie walked back around the counter like a little girl playing house. "What will you have?"

"Black coffee."

"Got it."

"So she's put you to work?" Sam stated the obvious.

"Not exactly. I volunteered. But we've been talking about it. I think she's working on a plan. You take cream?"

"No, just black. A plan—that sounds promising."

Sam was intrigued, but with his new frame of mind he found a table nearby and sat down, ready to sit and listen. He was relieved to have Shelly take control of her own situation. He didn't need to be the boss, and didn't want to be the boss.

Shelly came to the table and sat across from Sam. "Okay, here's the deal. The way I see it, Sea Siren is going to come in with their familiar concept. Their prices are high and they've always been high, but people line up there like robots anyway because they know what they're getting. They feel comfortable."

"And they feel like they're part of something cool," Sam said.

"Right, and I can't out-cool them. Plus, that might attract the tourists, but the locals don't care about cool."

"Uh huh."

"So, I've got the locals, but then the locals have their own coffee pots at home so they don't really need coffee either."

"So, if the locals don't care about cool, and they don't need coffee . . . sounds like you've talked yourself out of business." Sam took a long, slow, thoughtful sip of coffee.

Shelly scowled, realizing she'd talked herself in a circle, when the heavy sound of shoes scuffing on the porch signaled that Bo was coming in.

"Morning," he growled and ambled toward the counter, but slowed when he saw that Allie was there instead of Shelly. He cleared his throat to talk, but Allie spoke first.

"How are you feeling this morning, Bo?"

"Tired." He looked over his shoulder at Shelly, and she gave him a nod that said, "Go ahead," so he put his mug on the counter but without the usual clatter.

Allie twisted the lid off and turned to fill it up. The room was quiet but for the sound of coffee gurgling into the mug. Allie snapped the lid on and turned back to face her father. "This ought to get you going."

"She's not going to ask me if I want cream or nothing?" Bo looked at Shelly again.

"Cream? You? I just don't see it," Allie said.

"Smart girl." Bo took a sip and frowned. "A little weak, but it'll do." Bo looked around the room. "Where's that Dave feller?"

"Said he had to get back to Dallas," Shelly said.

"Dallas? I thought he lived around here. And as much as he's been around lately, I thought the two of you . . ."

"He lives in Dallas and he comes down here for vacation and that's all there is to it. Don't you have somewhere you need to be?"

"Yep, gotta check out the engine. I think Sam might have fouled up the throttle." And with that Bo was out the door.

"Did you see that?" Allie asked.

"Yes, that's your pa . . . I mean, Bo, every damn morning. It's his regular show. I oughta sell tickets," Shelly said.

"No, I mean, did you see how he came in and rattled your cage?"

"Yeah, but like I said, that's his regular deal. I guess I'm not getting it."

Sam interjected. "He poked you and provoked you. Strangers don't do that to each other."

"But families do that, and that's what the locals will come here for," Allie said. "That's why Bo comes here. Family. I've seen the way you all are. You're a family."

Sam and Shelly stared across the table at each other, pinned down by the weight of those words.

"Family, huh? I'm not so sure about that," countered Shelly.

"Then what made you all drop everything and go to Freeport to check on Bo?" Allie asked.

"We did that because he's our friend and because he

doesn't have family. Or we didn't know he did. But that's a lot different from being family."

"I don't know . . . some friends are closer than family, and some families aren't as close as friends. It's a fine line."

Shelly looked at Sam, and Sam nodded toward Allie. "Bo was right: smart girl."

Shelly pushed back her chair, stood up from the table and walked back to the counter. She pulled a damp rag out of the sink, wrung it out, and began scrubbing the counter hard. "Don't you all have some place you need to be?"

"I'm off today," Sam said. "And Allie . . . I thought she was with you?"

Shelly stopped scrubbing and scowled at Sam. "Why don't you take Allie with you, show her around or something."

"Okay." Sam motioned for Allie to come with him. They walked out the door and down the steps, Sam leading the way. Shelly shouted after them, "I'm still in charge here. It's still my name up on that sign, you know."

Sam and Allie were out of hearing range with Sam walking quickly and Allie trailing behind him as they turned the corner onto the main street. Sam was on autopilot, walking home out of habit, when Allie reached for his arm to slow him down.

"Where are we going?"

"Oh . . . sorry . . . I guess we're going to my place for a while."

Sam slowed his pace and Allie scooted up beside him. "I guess this was a bad idea for me to hang out here. Maybe I should catch a bus or something."

"Don't worry about it. Shelly just has a lot on her mind right now. We just need to give her a little space."

They continued walking in silence and in another ten minutes they turned the corner off the highway and into the trailer park. Sam twisted the handle on the trailer door and pushed it open for Allie to enter.

Allie stepped inside and when her eyes adjusted to the darkness, she saw that the trailer was clean and tidy even if it was small and cramped. "Nice."

"It's home. You want something? I've got water or orange juice, but that's about all." Sam motioned for Allie to sit at the little table.

"No, I'm okay. Maybe I'll just sit here for a little while and try to figure out what I should do."

Sam sat down across from her. "Well, I hope it doesn't take you as long as it's taken me. I've been working on that for almost two years."

"Really?" Allie looked at Sam, surprised by his confession.

"It's a long story." Sam turned and looked out the window.

"Is it true what I said back there . . . about you all being like family?" Allie asked.

"I think it depends on who you ask, and when you ask them." Sam turned back to face Allie. "I think we're all a little beat up, and people in that situation like to be alone sometimes. But it's also what we have in common, so I guess if there's a family connection, that would be it."

Now Allie stared out the window. She hadn't really thought of herself as being "beat up," but having met Bo and coming face-to-face with her own abandonment, she realized she might have that connection too.

Sam saw Allie's brow wrinkle and he tapped the table to get her attention. "Listen . . . you don't have to be a part of this. Our story doesn't have to be your story. You can go back to Freeport right now and forget that you ever met any of us and none of us will think the worse of you."

"Is that what you would do?"

"Well . . . it's what I did, and I don't know if it was the best solution. You can run from stuff but it has a way of following you anyway."

Allie stood up, stretched, bent over, and looked out the window. "The beach is that way, right?"

"Yep."

Allie walked out of the trailer and left Sam sitting at the table.

As evening fell on the town, Sam walked to the beach, expecting to find Allie sitting and thinking as he might do, but she wasn't there. He looked up and down the beach. A couple walked hand in hand, and a man jogged with a dog on the edge of the surf, but there was nobody else. He went back to the trailer and sat on the steps for a while, but when nine o'clock came and there was still no sign of Allie, Sam pulled on his shoes and walked back into town. When he got to the Dream Bean, he found the lights off and the door locked. He walked over to the *Cassie.* It too was dark, with the only sounds being the creak of wood and the clang of metal as the boat rocked gently on the water. Not knowing where Shelly lived or even her phone number, Sam went back to the Dream Bean and sat on the steps. Resting his chin in his hands, he wondered if he'd done it again—separated a father from his daughter.

Chapter 23

Sam was awakened by the jingle of keys. He opened his eyes to find Shelly standing over him.

"Waiting for me?" She jingled her keys again.

Sam straightened up and looked around. "Huh . . . what?"

Shelly stepped around him, unlocked the door, and walked into the Dream Bean. Sam stood up and looked around a moment and then followed her in.

"Did Allie come back to your house last night?" he asked.

"No. I thought she was with you . . . or Bo." Shelly could see the worry on Sam's face. "What happened yesterday afternoon?"

Sam explained how Allie had gone home with him and then walked to the beach and not come back.

"You checked the boat?"

"Yes."

"This morning?"

Sam walked out of the Dream Bean and down the sidewalk to the pier. As he approached the *Cassie* he could hear muffled voices coming from the pilothouse.

He stepped over the gunwale and followed the voices to the compartment behind the pilothouse where he found Allie and Bo seated on the cot, looking at photographs. Sam shuffled his feet and Bo looked up.

"Good Lord, scare the life out of a man why don't you," Bo growled.

Sam ignored Bo and stared at Allie.

"Sam . . . what is it?" she asked.

"You didn't come back. Where were you?"

"I walked on the beach for a while . . . and then I came here."

"But I looked. Nobody was here. Where were you?"

Allie looked at Bo and then back at Sam. "I guess you missed us. We went up the road to get something to eat."

Bo interjected. "Can't a man have a brew with his daughter without some beach bum's approval?"

"Yes . . . but . . ." Sam was flustered, his emotions flowing in every direction. "You just walked off and left."

Bo stood up. "Now listen here, mister. I appreciate your interest, but you can just mind your own business now."

Sam looked at Bo for the first time, and then back at Allie, his eyes red. He turned and walked out.

"That's right, go on back to your tin can," Bo said.

But Allie had seen the distress in Sam's eyes and followed after him. "Wait . . . Sam . . . I don't understand . . . wait."

Sam continued walking away.

Allie walked back inside where Bo was still sitting. "What is wrong with you? Why are you always so mean? Why can't you be kind just once?"

Allie didn't wait for an answer. She left the boat and ran up the pier to the street. She looked in every direction and when she didn't see Sam, she went to the Dream Bean and told Shelly what just happened.

"What am I missing here? What have I done wrong?"

"Sam's a sweet but . . . strange . . . man. He's got issues, but I don't know what they are."

"So what should I do?"

"I suppose you could go talk to him and just hash it out. I think he's working at the market today, but then there's no guarantee of that. He walked off the job once already."

"Really?"

"Like I said . . . he's a little strange."

"He's not strange. He's hurting." Shelly and Allie looked across the room to see Dave come in the door.

"Back from Dallas so soon?" Shelly asked.

"No, haven't left yet, but it looks like I've already missed something. What's up?"

The three of them sat down, and Allie and Shelly filled Dave in on the events of the past twenty-four hours. And then after some hesitation—and with some coaxing from Shelly and Allie—Dave told what he knew of Sam's crash in Dallas.

"No kidding? Wow, that would shake anyone up,"

Shelly said. "To have that hanging over his head . . . it's a wonder he didn't just walk off into the Gulf when he got here."

"And so yesterday he tried to be responsible and caring again, and well, you can sort of see why he's shaken," Dave said.

Allie shook her head. "I'm so sorry. I had no idea."

"It's not your fault," Dave said. "He has no claim on you, and you have every right to be as independent and aloof as he is."

Allie bristled. "Independent, sure, but aloof? Not hardly."

"Okay, wrong word. But independent . . ."

"That could describe any of us, including you." Shelly looked at Dave.

"That's probably true," he said.

Shelly gave Dave a questioning look. He ignored it and turned back to Allie. "You could go talk to him."

Allie thought about it a moment and then got up and left.

"Interesting girl. She has a thought and then she just gets up and goes without saying a word," said Shelly.

"Well, I need to go too, but not without saying something."

"Yes, and what would that be?"

"That I'm driving back to Dallas now and I'm not sure when I'll be back but . . ." He paused, not sure how to complete the sentence.

"But?" Shelly prompted.

"Let's just say that I definitely *will* be back and it will be sooner than later."

Dave stood up and Shelly walked him to the door and out onto the porch where his car was waiting.

"Packed?"

"Uh huh."

"Well then, have a safe trip and keep in touch."

"Definitely." Dave froze for a moment, unsure of whether to offer a handshake or a hug or neither. He settled on neither. "Well . . . see ya." He walked down the steps, got into his car, and drove away. Shelly went back into the Dream Bean with that word "definitely" lingering in her thoughts. It wasn't a word that she had heard much in her life. Everything—and everyone—seemed so fleeting.

A few blocks away, Allie walked into the market, and after asking around she found Sam in the storeroom loading a crate of apples.

"Sam, I'm so sorry I upset you. I didn't realize you'd be so worried. It's just . . ."

Sam picked up the crate and walked past Allie through the metal doors to the produce section. He set the crate down and started placing apples on the display.

Allie followed him. "Sam, please stop and talk to me."

"Shhh . . . you want me to lose my job? Wait for me outside. Please."

Ten minutes later, Sam found Allie sitting on a bench.

"I'm sorry I worried you, Sam."

Sam sat down next to her. "The silly thing is, I really don't know why I got so worried. I had no right. Besides . . . who are you to me? I didn't even know you until a few days ago."

"I really don't know you either . . . except I know you're a kind, caring man. I saw that in you when we first met at Bo's bedside and then on the boat. I should have been more considerate."

Allie paused. "On the other hand, Bo . . . oh my, is he a piece of work."

She laughed and Sam relaxed a little and let out a snicker.

"He risked his health to see you. That's no small thing." Sam stood up and stretched. "I better get back to work. I appreciate you coming to see me."

Allie stood too, and ignoring Sam's body language—his hands thrust awkwardly in his pockets—she placed a gentle kiss on his cheek. "See you later."

Sam pulled his right hand out of his pocket and cupped it against the glare of the sun as he watched her walk away.

Chapter 24

Dave leaned back in his chair and looked at the calendar. He did the math in his head again. "It's time."

"It's time for what?" came a voice from the next cubicle.

Dave sat up straight in his chair. He hadn't realized he had spoken out loud. He quickly looked at the clock. "Uh . . . time for lunch."

He texted Melody who worked in a cubicle on the other side of the floor: "Wanna eat?"

"Sure."

"See you downstairs."

Fifteen minutes later, as they munched on their favorite tacos, Dave broke the news.

"I'm leaving."

"What?" She almost dropped her food. "When . . . where?"

"Soon. I haven't given notice yet, but I will by the end of the week. As for where . . ."

Dave didn't have an answer for her. He really didn't have a clear answer for himself. The work he was doing no longer mattered to him, and it was time to free himself to do something that felt right. "I'm going to freelance," he said, not exactly sure what that meant.

"That's cool. I've always wanted to do that." But then Melody's enthusiasm faded, her brow wrinkled, and she leaned her head against her hand. "I hate this place. It's going to be unbearable without you."

"Naw, you'll be okay. Besides, this releases you from our pact."

They both laughed at the pact they'd made in jest: If they were both still at the business after the new product launch, they'd hold hands and jump in front of a commuter train. The launch was a month away, but Dave would leave before that.

"Well, I'm honestly happy for you, but I'm still bummed," Melody said.

Having announced his decision to one person, Dave had crossed a bridge for which there was no turning back. By telling Melody that he was leaving, he'd taken the first step to making it real. He knew she'd hold him to his decision and give him grief if he changed his mind. That night he sketched out a time line that began with giving notice on Friday, and continued with steps that he wouldn't tell anybody—not even Melody—just yet: He'd call the realtor who helped him and Debby sell their condo some years earlier and put his house on the market. And then, as quickly as possible, he'd return to Port Aransas and start looking for a place there.

Dave underlined that on the pad, and then drew a

box around it and then a double box. As he did so, it began to look and feel exactly like what his CPA had warned against: Don't do anything impulsive. That thought brought a wave of doubt, and he pushed the pad away, but then he pulled the pad back in front of him and did the math again. Twenty months had passed since Debby had died. He had given himself plenty of time to adjust and settle in to life alone. It was time to start planning a new life for himself. And at the moment, that life was in Port Aransas.

The next morning before going to the office Dave went to the cathedral a few blocks away. He wasn't a Catholic, but Debby had been and the great old church had been a place of solace and connection for him during the sorrowful days after her death. As usual it was almost empty in the early morning hours, and his feet echoed on the oak floors as he walked down the aisle and slid into a pew about halfway back from the white marble altar. Looking up at the stained glass windows with their depictions of disciples and saints, he tried to muster that feeling of closeness again, but this time he felt sadness and guilt. He felt like he was leaving her behind—as if her soul existed there and no place else.

Dave was wrestling with that thought when a child who was standing on the pew next to his mother, her head bowed in prayer, began making popping sounds and then little shouts, impressed with the sound of his own echo. Dave was envious, wishing he could shout too and release the pressure that had built up inside his heart. Instead, he spoke aloud the words that he had been carrying inside for months: "I'll love you always, but I can no longer hold you . . . and I need someone to hold. I'm still flesh and blood."

On the short walk to the office, Dave gathered his resolve, and, after stopping at his desk to put down his satchel and turn on his computer, he walked straight into the office of Roger, his boss, closed the door, and told him he was leaving.

"I wish you'd stay, but I'm not really surprised that you're leaving. I almost bolted this place when my parents died—even took a break for a while to get my head straight—but then I came back and settled in. You could do the same." It was, for Roger, a rare moment of personal connection.

Dave shook his head, and Roger leaned forward in his chair and took a more professional tone.

"So, here are your options: You can finish out the year and help us interview and hire your replacement, or you can leave immediately."

"Immediately?"

"Yes, as in today . . . right now."

Dave had not considered that possibility, but his answer came without hesitation. "I'll leave now."

For the next two hours he quietly straightened his desk and made a few notes for Roger or whoever might need them regarding the status of his projects. He'd never decorated his workspace with pictures and knick-knacks like some of the long-timers around him, so it took him no time at all to gather his few personal items into his beat-up satchel. Without saying anything to anyone, he quietly walked out of the building and climbed aboard the first train that pulled into the station in the next block.

As the train whisked him away from downtown, Dave felt the knot in his soul loosen and the muscles in his neck relax. He stared out the window at the passing landscape until the train entered the tunnel and the interior lights revealed his own reflection in the glass. The man staring back at him was a stranger—a tired veteran of the workday wars and not the young, vibrant recruit who had first hopped the train a dozen years earlier to take his place on the front lines of the corporate world. He turned his head away and closed his eyes until the train resurfaced and he felt the warm sunshine coming back through the glass. He didn't want to see that man again; he didn't want to be that man anymore.

By the end of the week, Dave had contacted the realtor about his house and had given the key to Jeff with instructions to collect his mail until he had a forwarding address.

"Hate to see you go, buddy, but I'm proud for you." Jeff slapped Dave on the back. "And I'm glad to know I'll have a couch to crash on if I ever get down to the beach."

Dave knew he was leaving a lot of personal business undone and a lot of things unsaid with other people he knew. There would be time to tie up those loose ends, even if it was from long distance. But right now, he was surrendering to the urge to "get out of Dodge." Packing little more than what he might take on a long vacation, he jumped in his car and began the long drive toward the coast.

As he drove south in the dark into the heart of Texas, Dave started to make plans in his head, trying to fill in the gaps of what might happen next. He could get a long-term corporate rate at the hotel on the highway, but he knew he'd need to conserve his resources for the long haul. He wondered if there might be another trailer available near Sam's, and the thought of that made him snicker. Imagine: being a neighbor in a trailer park with the former Dallas ad man. But then his mood lurched back to the serious side because while he didn't want to be the man staring back at him on the train, he also didn't want to be that man he met on the beach on that early morning of remembrance. So, who would he be? What would he do? He tried to convince himself that there would be time enough to figure it all out, but the strong vein of practicality that ran through his being flinched at the thought of being shiftless and adrift. No, that wouldn't do at all. That wouldn't be him either.

The sudden flash of lights from a truck coming over the hill toward him on the two-lane highway interrupted

Dave's thoughts. He was temporarily blinded, and when the truck had passed he regained his focus just in time to find himself in a tight curve down the backside of the hill. He tried to correct his angle but turned the wheel too sharply and spun out in the middle of the dark, deserted highway.

When his heart quit pounding and he realized he was okay, Dave slapped the steering wheel. "What am I doing? Why am I rushing? Nobody is expecting me to be anywhere. Nobody is waiting for me."

Dave turned the wheel until he was heading in the right direction again and drove down off the hill to where the highway flattened out and then he pulled onto the shoulder. He cut the engine and got out. It was dark and quiet except for the distant call of a night bird and the sound of livestock shuffling somewhere far away. He climbed onto the hood of the car and looked out over the dark valley for a moment, then lay back against the windshield. Above him the stars twinkled through a thin veil of clouds and the oaks and pines on the fence line rustled in the wind. The aroma of pine needles and fresh-cut hay filled his nostrils as he took in great, deep breaths.

Sometime later Dave awakened to the sensation of a damp film on his face. At first he thought it was a stray shower but the stars and moon above let him know it was just the early morning dew. Damp and shivering, he got back into his car and checked the time. It was 3:30; he had slept for three hours. For a moment he considered rolling back out onto the highway and making a dash for the coast. If he didn't stop, he could be on the beach in time for sunrise. But then he stopped himself again. There would be plenty of sunrises. No need to rush. He tilted his seat back and fell asleep again until the sound of a truck and the early morning light awoke him.

Dave turned back onto the highway and after another hour he rolled under Interstate 10 at Schulenburg and continued on into town where he spotted a small café with a couple of cars out front. He parked and walked inside. A young woman sitting at a table with some gray-haired men looked his way. "Just sit anywhere. You take coffee?"

"Yes, thank you."

Dave found a table near the window. A moment later the young woman put a cup of coffee and a menu on the table in front of him.

"You can choose from what's there, or we'll do different if you've got a taste for something else."

"Really?"

"Sure. But it takes longer once it gets busy."

Dave looked around. There were just four other people in the room.

"Oh, right now ain't nothing. An hour from now they'll be standing outside," she said.

"Really? I just passed a bunch of restaurants out on the interstate."

"Sure, but they don't got what we got."

"What's that?"

"We got Rusty. Like I said, he'll fix almost anything."

Dave scanned the menu, then closed it. "Okay, how about an omelet with two eggs, jack cheese, sausage, and avocados, and I'll take a side of hash browns. No, make that grilled rosemary potatoes."

"Coming right up," she said and walked away toward the kitchen.

The meal came prepared just the way Dave had ordered it. On top of that, it was hot and seasoned to perfection. As he ate and drank the stout coffee that the waitress kept pouring, he wondered how he had missed this place all these years. But then again, he reasoned, he'd been in too much of a hurry to notice. "Won't make that mistake again," he said to himself.

By the time Dave finished his breakfast, paid his check, left a generous tip and stepped outside, the dining room was full and so was the parking lot. Dave drummed the steering wheel as he turned back onto the street. He couldn't wait to see Shelly.

Chapter 25

Dave stretched as Shelly placed a mug of coffee in front of him. He was tired and achy from the trip back to the coast, especially from sleeping on top of the car. But he was nervous too. There was so much he wanted to tell Shelly, but he didn't know where to start or just how much to say. His worries were brushed aside quickly as Shelly started the conversation.

"So, Mr. Independent—I think that's what you called yourself when you left here hardly a week ago—what's the deal? Why are you back so soon?"

Dave fidgeted, cleared his throat, and then it all came out at once. "I quit my job and I'm moving to Port Aransas and I know how to save the Bean." And then there was silence as he and Shelly just stared at each other—he waiting for her response, and she trying to decide if she heard him correctly.

"Huh?" she said.

And instead of going back over what he'd just said, Dave threw on another layer, which surprised even himself. "And I like you a lot and want to know you better." His face flushed red, while across the table Shelly covered her mouth with both hands, her eyes big as saucers peeking over the tops.

"You're mad, you know?" she said finally. "Freakin' mad."

"Probably so, and . . . I think I said too much. I didn't sleep last night. This isn't really me."

"Oh . . . but I kind of like this version of you. More spontaneous, less buttoned down. But let's back up a little. Start with your job. You quit?"

"Yes. I wasn't going anywhere and I was tired of it. They'll get along fine without me. And . . . I don't really need to work right now. I have some unexpected savings . . . from Debby."

"So . . . you've quit and you're coming down here? You know . . . we really don't need another Sam in this town."

"Oh no, I'm not going to just hang out and do nothing. I've been thinking . . ."

"That's a little scary, but go ahead . . . what have you been thinking?"

Dave leaned forward and told Shelly about the café where he had breakfast completely off the menu. "It was amazing. It's like what Sam and Allie were talking about—a feeling of family. Like when you were a kid and you could sit down at the breakfast table and tell your mother what you wanted and she'd make it."

"And you think I should do that here? Just let people sit down and order off the ceiling or from some memory of home?" Shelly leaned back, crossing her arms.

"Well, not exactly like that. At this café, they were obviously limited by what they had on hand."

"And how am I going to do any of that without any staff or resources." Shelly raised her voice, which caused Dave to lean back in his chair too and put his hands in the air.

"Hold on. Calm down. I'm not talking about matching them exactly. But," he leaned forward again, "there might be parts of what they are doing that could be copied. Or at least that kind of spirit of belonging."

Shelly leaned forward, resting her cheek on her hands, her head cocked. In her mind she set aside all the business talk and went to that last item—Dave's clumsy confession that had all the poise of a junior high crush. She was now of an age where she wasn't sure how to react. She had no girlfriend standing ready to cover for her, to pass along a note that said, "Shelly asked me to tell you that she really likes you too." It was just her and this boyish man who was either drunk or exhausted or immature or . . . the word she was looking for was somewhere between goofy and adorable.

Finally, her thoughts arranged themselves into a sentence. "Regarding your other comment . . . I've enjoyed getting to know you a little and I look forward to getting to know you better. Now that you're planning to move to Port A, we'll have more time for that." She immediately realized how stiff that sounded and made her own awkward statement. "Oh, Dave, let's just roll with it, OK?"

"Sure," he said. He was relieved that she hadn't laughed out loud or told him to leave. Even so, neither Shelly nor Dave knew what to do next. They circled around each other with small talk while she got up to tend to the shop and he found little things to do to help, like straightening the counter. And then Dave regained his footing and suggested they reconvene the work group that had met just once to discuss the future of Shelly's Dream Bean but was interrupted by the trip to Freeport.

Word was spread around, and at six that evening they all gathered at the Dream Bean—Shelly, Dave, Allie, Bo, Sam—and Dave recapped what he had witnessed at the diner in Schulenburg.

"So here's what I think," he said. "We, uh, I mean Shelly, doesn't need to compete with Sea Siren. Instead, I think she needs to be something entirely different. I think the Bean needs to be a place where people will feel the way they want to feel when they are at home: appreciated, wanted, fussed over."

"Oh, she knows how to fuss all right," said Bo.

"That's not what I mean."

"I know what you mean, and I don't think she's got it in her."

Dave shook his head. "Sam . . . what do you think? You're the real expert here."

Sam was hesitant and uncomfortable. Unlike the last

time they met, he hadn't quite pulled himself up to the table as an equal. He wasn't sure if he felt hurt, or embarrassed, or a little of both. Finally, he spoke in the soft, hesitant voice that Shelly knew best.

"I don't know. I keep putting my nose where it doesn't belong. I'm not sure my opinion is worth much."

Shelly looked Sam straight in the eye.

"Sam . . . this is important to me . . . and your opinion does matter. If I know anything about you at all, it's that you care a lot; you're not frivolous. So I know that whatever you say, it's from the heart, and I trust and respect it. Please, Sam, I want your help. This shop is all I have. This and you." She looked around the table at all of them, and they all looked at Sam, waiting.

Sam stood up and with his hands shoved in his pockets he circled the room, looking about. He stopped and leaned against the counter, facing the others.

"It's an interesting idea. It usually doesn't happen by design. It's usually just because people ask for something different. At the moment, you don't really know if that's what people want."

"I'd like that," said Bo.

"You? But you never get anything but coffee," Shelly scoffed.

"That's just because all you ever have is cookies and those grainy muffins. I'd take a real breakfast every now and then if I knew I could have it."

Shelly leaned back in her chair, irritated.

"See, it's just a matter of knowing these things," said Dave.

"There's no guarantee." Sam spoke softly, making sure he was heard correctly. "Bo is just one person. But there's more to it than just getting people in. You'd have to buy right, price right, control inventory just so. Get any of that wrong and you could be in trouble in a hurry."

Shelly stood up, and she too began circling the room, but her tour was different from Sam's. He'd gotten up to clear his head and to eyeball the business, the room, the location. Shelly was looking at what she'd built—what she'd put into it and what was at stake. Nobody said anything for a moment as she walked about. Bo cleared his throat and began to make a gesture but Allie pulled his hand down and hissed a "shhhhh." Shelly didn't see any of that. She was standing at the windows, staring out beyond the boat masts to the open water where the white hull of a cruise ship shimmered in the evening light. She wondered what was out there, out beyond the narrow ribbon of coastline that she'd known all her life. Perhaps something better? And then the colored lights that Sam had strung across her porch that previous Christmas popped on with the timer, bringing her back to the Dream Bean and the life she knew. She walked back to the counter and leaned against it next to Sam.

"Let's do this."

Over the next two days everyone worked to get the

Dream Bean ready. Shelly and Allie went to the market and bought a dozen cartons of eggs, some bacon, biscuit mix, the basics. Dave and Sam, with hesitant approval from Shelly, went to a kitchen supply warehouse in Corpus Christi to scout out some equipment.

"That's fine, but don't you go and buy anything," Shelly said.

Shelly was furious when they rolled up to the Dream Bean six hours later pulling a rented trailer loaded with a used stove/grill combination, a mixer, a large capacity refrigerator, some other basic kitchen utensils, and sets of café dishes and stainless.

"Don't you two listen to anything?" she asked, standing on the porch as they pulled the tarp off the load. "I told you not to buy anything. I can't afford all of this."

She walked back into the shop, slamming the door behind her.

Sam and Dave looked at each other, and Dave shook his head. "I guess I better go work on this. Why don't you go see if you can find Bo? We'll need his tools."

Dave found Shelly in her usual state: furiously scrubbing the counter as if working on a stain that will never quite go away. He watched her for a moment, knowing that the wrong words would provoke her further. Finally, he knew he had to start with just two words: "I'm sorry."

"It's too much, it's too fast. I feel like things are out of control."

Dave reached for her arm, spun her around, and took her by the hand.

"Shelly . . . I'm sorry. I should have called you, but you would have said no and these are things you're going to need. As for paying for them . . . don't worry about that right now. You can pay me back some time. Or get it out of me through work. Or make me a partner . . . whatever arrangement suits you. I'd like it if you'd just accept this as a gift. Believe me, I didn't spend so much, and I was glad to do it. It's worth it to me. *You* are worth it to me."

Shelly looked into his eyes and noticed they were moist.

"Look at you," she said. "You're such a . . . ." She paused and shook her head, frustrated with him and ashamed at herself. "I'm sorry I got so angry. But please . . . just ask me next time you want to do something like this."

"But you'll say no."

"Not necessarily . . . you gotta give a girl a chance to at least think about it."

Shelly reached up to dab what she thought was a tear in the corner of his eye, and then without saying anything she wrapped her arms around him and hugged him. Dave was caught off guard, but not so much that he didn't hug her back and linger for a moment in that embrace. It had been so long since he had been that close to another human being and especially a woman —

close enough to hear her breath, feel her warmth, know her shape. He would have stayed there longer but Shelly let go.

"Okay," she said, "we better go find Bo because . . ."

"I already sent Sam for Bo and his tools."

"See, that's just what I'm saying, nobody waits for me." Shelly shook her head as she walked toward the door. They stepped out on the porch to find Bo and Sam sitting on the end of the trailer.

"What's the verdict? She gonna let us unload this junk?" Bo asked.

"Yes, and you better be careful with it, because it's not junk. It's my future," Shelly said.

Dave, Sam, and Bo spent the rest of the day carrying everything in and hooking it up while Shelly and Allie washed the dishes and utensils and took inventory. City code inspectors paid visits and made sure all the vents, exhaust fans, and fire extinguishers were in good working order.

Dave and Sam agreed to man the kitchen, with Dave leading the way having cooked at a burger joint in high school. "Breakfast is pretty easy," he reasoned. Sam would bus tables and wash dishes. Shelly would be out front, of course, since her name was on the sign. Allie would provide counter support and serve.

As for Bo, his role was pretty simple. On the appointed morning—an early Tuesday when there were a dozen or so people in for coffee and muffins—Bo walked in, set his metal mug down hard on the counter. Shelly filled it up. "What else?" she prompted him.

He looked puzzled for a moment, then had a moment of recollection, and in a booming voice said, "Why, Miss Shelly, I'd like . . ."

Shelly grabbed Bo's shirt collar and pulled him forward so his nose was almost touching hers. "Don't be so obvious. Just tell me what you want . . . in a regular voice. Just be you."

Bo straightened up. "Hmm," he said, scratching his chin for effect until Shelly stomped her foot. "Uh . . . I sure got a taste for a couple of scrambled eggs and some bacon. That would float my boat pretty good this morning."

"Coming up." She motioned him to go sit at a table. He shrugged a question. "Just anywhere," she pleaded.

A few minutes later, the smell of bacon began to fill the room, and a short while after that Allie carried a plate of real food out to Bo's table.

"Looks great," he said.

"Just holler if you need anything else."

The exchange caught the attention of everyone in the room, and soon a woman was at the counter asking to see a menu.

"Oh, we don't have anything written down, but if there's something you want we'll try to fix it," Allie said, repeating almost exactly what Dave had heard at the diner in Schulenburg. Others followed and before long

Allie was carrying out plates of bacon, toast, hash browns, and mixed fruit. Allie and Shelly wrote up the tickets from a rough price list that Dave had calculated to allow just enough margin to cover the costs and put a little extra in the cash drawer. By eleven that first morning, business tapered off and Dave gathered everyone at a table to debrief.

"So . . . how are you feeling?" He looked at Shelly, who leaned over the table with her face buried in her arms.

"Wrung out," she said, her voice muffled, but when she raised up she couldn't hide a big smile. "That was so cool."

"Yes," Allie said, clapping her hands.

"I'm gonna get fat eating like this," Bo said, but Allie reminded him that it wasn't his "job" to come in every day and eat. To which Shelly added, "And it's not going to be free all the time either."

Bo huffed, while Dave looked at Sam, who was turning his head on his shoulders to loosen muscles that were stiff from leaning over the sink all morning. "Well, what do *you* think?"

"I think we had a good first day," Sam said. "And now we better make sure we've got enough food for tomorrow. The second day will be even busier."

"Smart man," Dave said, getting up and patting Sam on the back. "Shelly, let's check the fridge and see what we need to replenish."

Dave, Shelly, and Allie all walked to the back, leaving Sam and Bo alone. Neither said a word for a moment, and Sam stood up to see if there were any tables that needed cleaning.

"You done good," Bo said finally.

"What's that?"

"This restaurant idea. You . . . all of you really . . . have done good for Shelly. She's needed something good to happen."

Sam just nodded as he straightened chairs. "Everyone's pitched in. Besides, it was Dave's idea."

"Yeah, but you encouraged her. Dave, he means well but those two are a little goofy on each other, so she needed an honest opinion from someone."

"Suppose so."

"Well, guess I better go tend to my business." Bo waited for a response, but when Sam didn't reply, Bo walked out the door.

"Tell 'em we're fresh out," Shelly shouted from the back when she heard the bells rattle on the door. When there was no response, she walked out front.

"Oh, I thought . . ."

"It was just Bo leaving. Said something about tending to business."

"Yes, I guess that's right," she said. "You can run on too if you need to."

"I'm not due at the market till 2:30. I'll help clean up the kitchen."

"That's okay, why don't you go rest a while before your shift. You've gotta be exhausted."

"Thanks, I think I will." Sam untied his apron and folded it and handed it to Shelly.

She took it, then pulled him forward and gave him a hug, the second one she'd given that week.

"Thank you, Sam."

"You bet," he said softly.

Walking down the highway to the trailer, Sam felt a heaviness that at first he thought was fatigue or maybe the start of a cold or the flu. He'd been running hard in recent days, helping get the Dream Bean ready while keeping his hours at the market. Anxious to get some rest, he picked up his pace and was almost running by the time he turned into the trailer park and reached his door. Inside, he emptied his pockets, kicked off his shoes, and climbed onto the bed for an hour's nap.

Sam was almost asleep when the distant sound of the ferry horns washed over him and gave him a chill. He reached down to pull the tattered blanket up over his chest when he realized what the heaviness and chill were about. Bo had put it into words—Dave and Shelly were "a little goofy on each other"—and Shelly had punctuated it when she hugged Sam the way a friend or daughter would. Sam moaned out loud because he knew that the heaviness he felt was jealousy. Not jealousy in that he had a desire for Shelly, but a jealousy of that closeness that Dave and Shelly were beginning to enjoy.

It had been so long since Sam had known that. He was battered and bruised now, but he wasn't old yet. And he was still a man. As the ferry horns cried out again, tears welled up in his eyes.

Chapter 26

Business at the Dream Bean continued at a strong pace over the next few days. The locals took to the new scheme well, with most sticking to what would be considered a normal American breakfast, while a few conjured up plates that came from some unknown place in their background. Such as a woman who asked for an omelet with crawfish. When asked about it, she said her grandmother used to make it that way in Louisiana.

"We don't stock crawfish, but we can throw in some black olives," Allie offered.

"No, wouldn't be the same. Just give me ham and cheese."

But then a few people had trouble with the concept. One morning Hap, an old fisherman, came in and stood at the counter, frozen with indecision. As the line grew longer behind him, Allie tried to prompt him by naming off eggs in different styles, pancakes and waffles, bagels and muffins.

That confused Hap even further, and when Shelly walked by and saw the line stringing toward the door, she took charge.

"C'mon now, Hap, just make a decision. Close your eyes, think of home, and name something."

Hap closed his eyes and screwed up his face. "Porridge."

"Then porridge it is." Shelly scribbled "oatmeal" on the order pad.

"But . . . I was just kidding."

"I wasn't," Shelly snapped. "You can come back tomorrow and try again. I'm sure something better will come to mind. Meanwhile, that'll be a dollar."

"A dollar . . . for a bowl of porridge? Forget it. I'm going home."

"Have it your way. Next."

And so it went over the next few weeks. Shelly was positively beaming, her sharp tongue softened by a slight smirk and a wink. Everyone noticed, and nobody more so than Dave who was drawn to Shelly more and more. They were together all day every day, working, eating, and—as couldn't be missed—laughing.

"They'll be slobbering all over each other pretty soon," Bo grumbled one morning.

"Oh leave 'em alone. I think it's sweet," said Allie. "We should always be happy when friends find love."

"What do you say, Sam?" Bo asked. "You got an opinion about this love business?"

Sam, who was taking a break before going to the market, didn't want any part of the conversation, but Bo kept pushing until he finally spoke.

"I agree with Allie."

"Oh listen to you, like you know something about love," Bo scoffed.

"I know more than you think, and more than I'll ever tell. Besides . . . I didn't run away from it like you did."

"That's not what I hear," Bo said coldly.

Sam pushed his chair back, stood up, and walked toward the door.

"Look, he's retreating," Bo said.

"No, just going to work. Something you haven't done in years." Sam stopped at the door and then turned and looked back across the room at Shelly.

"I may be a little late tomorrow. We're stocking for SandFest at the market."

"Oh . . . thanks for reminding me," Shelly said, her eyes getting big. "I've gotta go shopping too."

Dave stood up straight like a dog detecting the rustle of an unseen intruder. "SandFest, what's that? Is that what they call spring break here?"

"No, spring break was while you were in Dallas," Shelly said. "It's not as big here as down on South Padre Island. But SandFest—that's much bigger and brings in everything from families to party animals."

Bo growled. "You got that animal thing right."

Allie giggled. "Sounds like fun to me."

"Depends on your idea of fun," Shelly said. "If you don't mind being mauled by cross-eyed drunken college boys then you might enjoy it."

"Like I said . . . sounds like fun." Allie tried but failed to keep a straight face.

"They'll have to get around me first," Bo said, and then he was out the door like Sam.

Shelly left Allie to run the Dream Bean that afternoon so she could stock up on groceries. Dave went back to his hotel and stopped at the desk to ask about SandFest traffic.

"We're gonna be full, but it's mostly families here," said the desk clerk.

Dave was relieved, but he wasn't looking forward to the wave of families and their own type of noise. He had enjoyed the relative quiet of the hotel during the off-season and hadn't given any thought to what the warm weather would bring. Realizing that SandFest would be just the beginning of a full summer of screaming children and slamming doors, Dave stopped at a convenience store and picked up the local real estate paper. Back at the Dream Bean he poured himself a cup of coffee and sat down at a table to scan the listings. Allie had nobody to wait on so she dropped into a chair beside him.

"Thinking about making it permanent?" she asked.

"Permanent? Right now I'm just looking to get out of the hotel. I'm not sure what permanent means just yet." Dave's eyes reached the bottom of the page and started working up the next column, but he was distracted by Allie's gaze.

"You know . . . I'm not planning to stay with Shelly

forever," Allie said. "I've been doing my own looking, and if I move out that would free up a room at her place. Not that you necessarily need your own room . . ."

"Whoa now, you're moving a little fast there, Allie." Dave quit pretending to read the paper and looked her in the eye. "We're having a nice time getting to know each other, but nobody is gonna start shacking up."

"Okay, okay. But I have been looking, so she may have another room soon."

Dave leaned back in his chair and crossed his arms. "I've been wondering what your long-term plans are. Don't you have friends back in Freeport? And what about your job?"

"In case you haven't noticed, I've been AWOL for six weeks. Actually, I called Walmart a good while back and told them I quit."

"Well that explains that. But what about friends?"

Allie rested her chin on her hands. "There's nobody there I'm missing . . . or who's missing me."

"Hmm . . . that's pretty much the way I've been feeling too." Dave tore the paper down the middle and gave half of it to Allie. They were sitting there quietly, reading, when Shelly came in through the back door with two full bags of groceries.

"What's up?" she asked.

"I'm going to stay," Allie said, still looking down at the paper.

"Stay?" Shelly set the groceries down.

"Yes, in Port A."

Allie and Dave watched as Shelly's expression turned from puzzlement to concern.

"So . . . where are you going to . . ."

Allie laughed out loud before Shelly could finish. "Don't worry, I'm not going to move in with you permanently. I've already looked around a little in my free time. There are a few good possibilities."

Shelly tried to hide the relief on her face, but then she saw Dave's smirk and she couldn't hide her irritation. "So you're in on this, too."

"No, no, she just told me about it," Dave said. He got up, stretched, and then gave Shelly a playful bump with his shoulder as he walked past her to help put up the groceries.

"More bags in the car," Shelly shouted at Dave, and then turned back to Allie, hands on her hips.

"Okay then, little sister, how can we help you?"

"Well, for starters you can answer an obvious question."

"What?"

"Do I have a job here . . . a paying job . . . or do I need to start looking for work, too?"

"Oh . . . yes . . . of course." Shelly blushed. "I've been meaning to talk to you about that. With business the way it's been, I've got a little room in the budget for part-time help. It might not pay your full rent when you find a place, but it'd get you halfway there."

"Halfway's fine."

"Then it's a deal," Shelly said, and what started as an awkward, business-like handshake melted into a hug. Shelly's voice grew soft, her eyes moist. "I was hoping you might be thinking about staying."

"But just not with you, right?" Allie laughed.

"Oh stop it." Shelly reached out to swat at Allie, but the younger girl dodged her and ran to the kitchen to help with the groceries.

"Interesting development," Shelly said to Dave while Allie was out of hearing range.

"Yes, and you should hear what she suggested for me and you." Dave grinned.

Shelly rolled her eyes and didn't dare ask what it was, but she knew. Allie moving out of her house meant an empty room. She wasn't ready for anything like that, and while she didn't think Dave was either, she wasn't going to test the waters and ask him. And she didn't have to. On Monday morning Dave announced he had moved out of the hotel and into a small, furnished duplex not far from the Dream Bean. A few days later, Allie made a similar announcement: she'd found a bungalow that would be available in a few weeks, and it was just down the street from Dave.

"Good, you can pester her instead of me," Shelly said to Dave, but everyone knew she was enjoying the attention.

Chapter 27

Sam awoke to the puttering of diesel engines and crunching of tires on the sand-dusted blacktop outside his trailer. He sat up in bed and looked out the window to see a line of flatbed trucks loaded with tents, tables, metal barricades, and portable toilets.

"Damn fest," he muttered and lay back down in bed. It was just Monday morning, and already Sam was feeling like a prisoner inside his trailer. While the event only lasted three days, it took longer than that to set up, and it all took place on the beach—his beach—just outside the trailer park. And while spring break might draw sixty thousand people to the island, it was spread up and down the beach and all around the town over a two-week period. But SandFest could bring a hundred thousand for three intense days right outside his door.

Sam was still grumbling when he got to the Dream Bean and put on his apron.

"What's up?" Dave asked.

"SandFest."

"Well, why don't you come stay with me till it's over? You can sleep on the sofa."

"Uh . . . I don't know."

"Oh come on, it'll be good for you. You'll be closer to work and you'll definitely get in some extra hours here and at the market."

"I'd do it, Sam," said Shelly. "I wouldn't want to be anywhere near that circus."

"Sounds fun to me," said Allie.

"That's just because you've never been," said Shelly.

"Well, I for one plan to check it out."

"Me too," said Dave. "So, what about the bed, Sam?"

"I appreciate it, but I think I'll just tough it out."

"Suit yourself." Dave turned back to Allie. "Let's go down Friday afternoon."

"Better make it Sunday," Shelly said. "That's when they do all the judging."

"Let's make it Saturday," said Allie. "I want to watch them making the sculptures."

"It's a date." Dave looked at Shelly and gave her a sly wink.

Business around the piers picked up as preparations for SandFest moved along. Shelly and Allie were alone at the shop that Thursday afternoon when a small group of college kids came in dressed for the beach. They crowded around the counter, shouting their orders in random order, punctuated by "no" and "wait," until Allie parked her pad and pen on the counter. Noticing Allie's frustration, one of the boys—a tall, handsome redhead—came to her rescue.

"C'mon guys, let's get organized. One at a time."

It was then that Allie noticed the kids were ordering as couples and then backing away to a table in the middle of the room. All but the redhead, who was last to order.

"I'll have a large iced tea. Sorry about the others. They've been out of control since we got here."

"Where you from?"

"Nacogdoches."

"Well that explains it."

"Explains what?"

"You're from so deep in the woods that you don't know what to do when you get out in the sunshine."

He laughed. "Yes ma'am, I reckon that's probably right."

"And you can put away that 'ma'am' nonsense," Allie said. "I'm not any older than you, if at all. And I do have a name."

"And what's that?" he asked as he handed over his credit card.

"Allie." She swiped the card and noted his name as she handed it back. "I'll bring it out to you all in a moment, Justin." Allie smiled.

Justin went to join the others and Allie filled the order. Shelly noticed the little bounce in Allie's step and sidled up next to her. "I didn't take you as favoring redheads."

"Oh stop it. That boy's a total stranger."

"Yeah, well, so was Dave when he first stood at this counter."

Allie gave Shelly a look that said, "You really want us to start talking about you and Dave?" Shelly realized her blunder and turned away to take care of other chores.

Allie loaded up a tray with iced teas and iced coffees and carried it over to the table. As she walked away, one of the boys whistled through his teeth, and the others laughed. Allie went back to the counter where Shelly was watching—and listening. The language at the table had grown crude, and while Shelly's ears were not at all tender, she'd heard enough when one of the boys said to the redhead, "You definitely should get you some of that island skank."

Shelly marched to the table. "I don't mind you kids being here, but I don't like that language. Shut it up or leave."

"Well now, aren't we tough," said one of the boys.

"Oooh, gonna go call the boss and have him bounce us?" asked a girl in mock fear.

Allie snickered from across the room. She knew what was coming next.

"No, I'm not gonna call the boss. I *am* the boss, and I'll tell you one more time: Clean up your language or get out of *my* shop."

Shelly turned to go back to the counter, but wheeled around again when she heard one of the girls mutter, "Testy old bitch."

"That's it," Shelly said. She walked to the door and held it open with her body. "Get out . . . now!"

"Now wait a minute . . . ," one of them said, but Allie, walking to the table, cut her off: "You better do what she says."

"You too?" said another girl, and then to one of the others, "Like mamma bitch, like daughter bitch."

Allie reached into the middle of the table, picked up a tall cup, popped off the lid, and splashed its icy contents in the girl's face. "I may be a bitch, but you're a sloppy mess. Better go back to the hotel and clean up."

The girl was speechless as she wiped her eyes clear with her hands. Allie pointed to the door. They all got up in a hurry, knocking over chairs and muttering as they retreated to the door.

"I told you we should've gone to Houston instead of this hick town," said one of the boys loudly.

Justin was the last out the door. His face flushed with embarrassment. "I'm sorry," he said to Allie in a hushed voice so the others couldn't hear. He shrugged and smiled, and Allie waved and followed him out onto the porch.

"Sorry to break up the party. That one at least seemed nice," Shelly said.

Allie sighed as she leaned against the porch rail, watching the kids walk away until they turned the corner. "I better mop up."

Nothing more was said about the incident, but on

Saturday after the rush Shelly handed Allie a small white envelope. "This was in the mailbox."

Allie looked at the front and saw her name scribbled in pencil. Inside was a handwritten note on a page torn from a motel notepad: "Sorry we were rude. Like U said—too much sunshine. C U sometime? Justin." And then he added an email address.

Allie let a small giggle slip past her lips as she stuffed the note in her pocket.

~ ~ ~ ~ ~

"Well, you ready to go?" Dave had gone home and come back wearing shorts and a T-shirt and sandals.

"Sure. Just a second." Allie disappeared to the back and came out in shorts, a bikini top, and flip-flops.

"Sure you won't come with us?" Dave asked Shelly.

"Naw, been there done that."

"She's no fun. Come on." Allie pulled Dave by the hand out the door.

Allie and Dave wandered from station to station on the beach where artists of every age and description chiseled away at great mounds of sand. There were mermaids, sea creatures, and tall turreted castles, as one would expect, but also renditions of things you'd never equate with the sea: A giant bust of Willie Nelson clutching his guitar, an elephant dancing with a monkey, dogs at a table playing cards.

"Crazy. Fantastic." Allie offered critiques of every

new creation. "I've never seen anything like it." And just as quickly as she was drawn into a scene, walking around it to take in every little sculpted detail, her attention was drawn away by a group of kids walking by.

Dave noticed her standing on her tiptoes. "Think he might be here?"

"Who?"

"That redheaded boy I heard about."

"Maybe."

Dave started to laugh and Allie gave him a push toward one of the sculptures.

"Careful," he said, keeping his balance as his leg brushed against the rope surrounding a giant likeness of a dragon eating a man.

"And what about you?" Allie asked. "Disappointed that Shelly didn't come?"

"A little. But she does her own thing and that's something I like about her. She's not a follower."

"Then you're the one that'll have to do the chasing and catching." Allie gave Dave another teasing shove and then ran off to the next sculpted scene. And on they went past the contest sand carvings and then to the area set aside for children and families to try their hand. Allie took off her flip-flops and waded ankle deep into the surf to cool her feet. And then she stood a moment, looking back toward the crowd, unconsciously drawing in the damp sand with her toes.

"Going to draw something?" Dave asked.

"No, just playing. You can go on back if you wish, but I think I'll stay out here awhile."

"Okay. I might go back and see if Shelly needs help cleaning up."

Allie smiled. "You do that." She hesitated. "You know . . . even a girl like Shelly likes being chased a little."

Chapter 28

With the SandFest storm safely gone, life returned to normal at the Dream Bean and all up and down Mustang Island. That included getting things ready for summer tourists. At Sea Siren, which was putting the finishing touches on its store in a new strip center at the busy corner of the road leading into town from the ferry landing, Karl Dexter was overseeing the finish-out and the hiring of managers and assistants.

He was standing outside one cool early May morning, taking a cigarette break, when he noticed Sam walking up from the Dream Bean and around the corner toward the market. Karl tossed his cigarette onto the sidewalk and stepped on it as he crossed the street.

"Excuse me, aren't you . . . ," he started, but Sam was in no mood for strangers and ducked his shoulder and slid by without making eye contact.

"You work with Shelly," Karl persisted, which caused Sam to stop and turn.

"Yes?"

"It's just . . . I recognize you from the Dream Bean."

"Yes." Sam tried to be polite, but he needed and

wanted to keep moving. He was late for his shift at the market.

"From what I can tell business is going well."

Sam nodded.

"And I'm told you're one of the architects of that success?"

"Where'd you hear that . . ."—the irritation rose in Sam's voice—". . . and just who are you?"

"Oh, sorry. I'm Karl Dexter. I'm from Sea Siren. Corporate office. You've probably heard of me. Your partner Shelly threw me out a few months back."

Sam looked across the street at Sea Siren and then back at this man and put it together in his mind. Karl was the corporate advance man who had annoyed Shelly's customers with his loud cell phone conversation, and then drew the ire of Shelly when he dared to offer her advice.

Karl stuck out his hand, but Sam kept his stuffed in his pocket.

Karl continued: "I've been real impressed . . . and I was wondering if we could talk business some time."

"We don't have anything to talk about. It's not my business; I'm not Shelly's partner. Sorry, but I'm late." Sam turned and walked away, leaving Karl standing on the corner.

Later that evening, Sam was in his trailer, heating a can of soup when he heard the door rattle, and then there was a sharp knock. Visitors were rare, and Sam stood still for a moment to see if it was just the wind, or if not, then perhaps the visitor would leave. But there was another knock, so Sam turned down the burner and went to the door. He swung it out slowly to find Karl standing on the gravel below the step.

"Mind if I come in for a moment," Karl said, drawing on a cigarette and then dropping it onto the ground.

"I told you we have nothing to talk about," Sam said, but reading Karl's face, he could tell this man was not going to just walk away, so he motioned him in with a resigned, "Okay."

Karl stood in the middle of the trailer and looked around for a moment until Sam motioned him to sit at the table. "Cozy little place you got here."

Sam dropped into the other seat and didn't say a word. It was Karl who had come with something to say.

"Okay, here's the situation." Karl explained that after the incident at the Dream Bean, he had dispatched his corporate researchers to come to town as tourists and gather information about the Dream Bean. They took note of customer counts, menu offerings, and, most recently, the lack of a menu.

"Pretty slick, if you ask me," Karl said, thumping the table with his knuckles.

Sam didn't change his expression, so Karl continued. "We also got pictures of Shelly and everyone who worked at the shop, and with a little research . . . well, we found out who you are."

Again, Sam didn't say a word.

"You don't seem surprised."

"Nope, I did my share of market research in the past."

"Okay," Karl continued, "we knew that, too. So, here's my proposition: We're exploring a new concept—a larger breakfast menu—and we think you'd be just the right person to whip it into shape and launch it. You could work from wherever you want to, with all the perks and a nice six-figure salary to start on."

By this time, Sam had quit looking Karl in the eyes and instead was looking at his own hands, the rough sunburned skin, the chipped nails, the sloppy cuticles. They weren't handsome hands, but they were honest hands.

Sam looked up at Karl and gave his answer. "That's all in my past. I don't need that type of stress, and I know I don't have the energy for that anymore."

"You sure I can't change your mind?"

"Nope."

"Well then, okay." Karl thumped the table with his knuckles again and stood up to leave. He turned to take one last look. "Cozy place."

Just as the door closed behind Karl, Shelly turned into the trailer park and saw him walk from Sam's trailer toward a bright red Audi. Shelly was coming, unannounced, with Sam's paycheck and some food, but when she saw Karl's face—one she could never forget—

she drove past him and circled back through the trailer park, her mind spinning as she considered what she had just seen. When she came back toward the entrance and Sam's trailer, she put her hand on top of the foil-wrapped food sitting in the passenger seat and hit the accelerator hard. Inside the trailer, Sam heard the spin of tires and the ping of gravel on metal as he stirred his pan of soup.

For the next two days there was a distance between Shelly and Sam—their conversation was short and to the point—but neither one knew the full measure of why.

Sam didn't know that Shelly had seen Karl leave his trailer, and now she was thinking the worst of him—that perhaps he was considering tossing aside their friendship and going to work for Sea Siren. While that didn't seem like something Sam would do, Shelly's doubts about how well she knew him began to grow out of proportion until she was convinced in her own mind that Sam had been waiting for the right opportunity to go back to the corporate world. She'd seen him go from a beach bum to a more polished man in khakis and sport shirt. Wouldn't a coat and tie be just another step in his revival?

Dave noticed Shelly's cloudy disposition and casually asked, "What's up?" But she said nothing more than that she was feeling a little tired. And it was an honest answer because the stress of worries and unanswered questions was keeping her awake at night.

What Shelly didn't know was that Sam had not

invited Karl's attention and that he had no desire to go back to the corporate world—not even for a six-figure salary. The sullen expression she saw on his face, which she interpreted as him trying to mask his guilt, was actually fatigue from trudging through the sadness of the past once more. While Karl had only spoken of Sam's success, his mention of that had pushed Sam into reliving once more his fall from grace. Shortly after Karl left the trailer and Shelly sped away, Sam had turned off the stove and walked out onto the moonlit beach where he contemplated walking straight out into the Gulf until the waves covered his head and he could gulp in the salty water until he was finally free. But instead he sat down in the sand and let himself be hypnotized into a sort of empty stupor by the endless rolling of the breakers. He might have stayed there deep into the next day if an early-morning trash truck hadn't forced him onto his feet and out of the way. As it was, when Shelly saw Sam the next day, he was in the grip of a deep-to-the bone emotional and physical fatigue. His lack of focus just heightened Shelly's fear that Sam was guilty, and when he failed to move quickly to clean up some tables, she snapped at him.

"If you can't handle the work, then just go home . . . or better yet, go someplace that you find more exciting, because this is as good as it gets around here," Shelly said.

The sharp words caused everyone within hearing

range to stop in their tracks, especially Allie and Dave. Allie raised a questioning eyebrow at Dave, and he just shrugged back.

Sam, who thought that he was being chastised for his fatigue, quietly took off his apron and left the Dream Bean, choosing to walk home by way of the beach rather than the highway. He didn't want to be anywhere near Sea Siren.

Dave confronted Shelly. "What's going on between you two? You haven't spoken to each other in days. We've all noticed the change."

"I don't know," Shelly said. "Maybe you should go ask Sam. He's the one hiding secrets."

"Secrets? What secrets?" For the first time, Dave was irritated at Shelly's cold, accusatory air. "The man holds a lot inside, but what secrets could he possibly have that would mean anything to you?"

"Oh . . . I think he has plenty, but since you know the man so well, why don't you go down to the trailer and ask him yourself. Or better yet, go over to Sea Siren. You might even find him there."

"What the hell are you talking about, Shelly? You're not making any sense at all."

But Shelly wouldn't answer and turned back to her work. By closing time, the whole shop was in a quiet boil with nobody talking and nobody really knowing why. And what none of them knew was that Sam's rejection of Karl had provoked Karl into action. A few blocks away,

Sea Siren opened with a grand celebration and a new breakfast menu they had never tried anywhere else. And because none of the local regulars at the Dream Bean would ever step inside Sea Siren, Shelly and her crew had no way of knowing what was going on. Until one morning when Allie strode in with a large clear Sea Siren cup in her hand and set it on the counter as she put away her purse and reached for an apron.

Shelly turned around and saw the cup on the counter and her jaw dropped. "Is that? . . . Traitor!"

"Oh, stop it. It's just a mocha latte . . . and it's really not very good." Allie tossed the cup into the trash. "But you better look at this." She pulled a folded piece of green paper out of her hip pocket and handed it to Shelly, who opened it up to find a breakfast menu with the words "Coming Soon" splashed across the top.

"That does it." She walked hard back into the kitchen where she found Sam scrubbing a pot. She slapped the paper onto the worktable. "What the hell is this?"

Sam turned off the water and dried his hands on his apron and then picked up the sheet. "It's a menu."

"Yes, a menu . . . from Sea Siren."

Sam looked at it again. "So, they're going to serve breakfast."

"But Sea Siren doesn't do food like that. They never have, but now they are."

"And . . . is there a law against that?"

"No . . . but don't you think it's a little strange that

they should start up with food after . . . " Shelly paused. She wasn't sure whether to come right out and accuse Sam, or wait for him to confess.

"Shelly, I'm really too tired for guessing games. Why don't you go ahead and just tell me what you're getting at."

Forced to take the next step, Shelly let it all out.

"Dammit, Sam, you had that man from Sea Siren over at your place, and the next thing I see is a menu that looks a lot like the menu we would have if we had a menu. But the point is that they're going to serve food now and there's no way we can compete with them."

Sam leaned back against the worktable, dumbstruck by Shelly's accusation. He held the menu in his damp fingers. "And you think I have something to do with this?"

"Well, what am I supposed to make of it? You meet with the man and then the next thing I know he's doing what we're doing."

"Meet with the man? He came uninvited and knocked on my door. He threw a crazy proposition at me and I told him 'no' and he left. Do you really think I would conspire to hurt you with something like this?"

With her anger and doubt finally released, Shelly's shoulders slumped and she wrapped her arms around herself as if trying to hold herself together. She spoke softly now. "I'm just so frightened, Sam. I don't know who or what to believe."

Sam shook his head. "Shelly, there's nothing I would ever do to hurt or harm you. You . . . all of you . . . but especially you . . . you're all I have."

Sam looked at the menu again and a wave of understanding washed over him. He took Shelly by the hands and looked into her eyes.

"It's true, Shelly, I *have* hurt you. It was unintentional, but I know what I have to do."

"How can I help?"

"You can't. I'm the only one who can fix this."

Sam took off his apron and walked briskly out the door and up the street. He picked his way through the heavy traffic at the corner and pushed through the doors of Sea Siren, where he stepped past the short line of customers and addressed a young barista working on an order.

"I need to see Karl Dexter."

"Oh, he's not seeing anyone today. All the positions have been filled."

"I'm not here for an interview. Please, just tell him that Sam is here to see him. He'll know who I am."

The young girl slipped through a door and a moment later came back out and motioned for Sam to follow her to a small office where Karl was looking at a computer screen. Before he could stand up for a greeting, Sam made his pitch.

"Listen, Shelly and her friends are just trying to make a living. They don't want to compete with you. Your market is completely different. We're mostly local, and you're going to have the tourists. I think we can get along fine if we just stick to our own markets."

"What, no winner take all?"

"Not from us. If we can make enough to pay the bills, then we're satisfied."

Karl leaned back in his chair and cupped his hands behind his head. "I don't know. Our philosophy is different, Sam. We like to win by . . . winning. Stomping the competition, actually. We don't really believe in win-win."

"Yeah, I know how that goes, but when you play that way you end up losing eventually."

"What makes you so sure?"

Sam spoke softly. "I didn't always live in that trailer, you know."

"Yes, I know."

"So, can we call a truce? You stick to your regular concept, and let us do our local thing?"

Karl thought about it for a moment and then stood up. "Only if you'll accept my handshake this time."

Sam stuck out his hand.

Chapter 29

"I need help," Allie announced one morning in mid-May.

"Help? What help?" Bo asked with an uneasy tone. He had embraced being this girl's father, but he was short on fatherly skills and for him the word "help" meant there was some work ahead. In this case, his instincts were correct.

"I've signed a lease, and I need help moving my stuff from Freeport," she said.

"Sure, when do you want to move?" Dave asked.

"As soon as any of you can take a day off. I don't have much to haul, but I'll probably need a small truck for the bigger furniture."

"We could lighten the load. I've got a car," Dave said.

"Sure, that'd be cool."

It was decided that Dave and Allie would drive his car to Freeport where Allie would rent a truck. Sam, who had let his license lapse and didn't want to renew it, would stay behind and help Shelly run the Dream Bean.

Everything was set until Bo heard the plan.

"That's nonsense. You don't need a truck. We'll just

bring it all back on the *Cassie*. She's got plenty of room on her deck and we can just float it all right back up here."

"We'll still need a trailer or pickup to get it from the pier to Allie's place," Dave said.

"We can borrow a trailer. They're parked in alleys all over town," Bo said.

Allie thought about it a moment. "Fine, but we're still going to need at least one car for hauling some stuff. I'm not going to risk all my valuables on that nasty old boat."

So the new plan was for Dave and Allie to drive up together and start packing, while Bo made the voyage up the coastline. And with insistence from the others, including Shelly, Sam was pulled into the packing trip as well.

Sam wasn't keen on the trip to Freeport, especially with Bo throwing his weight around. Of all his new Port Aransas "family," Bo was the hardest for Sam to warm up to. There was a side of Bo that reminded Sam of his previous self—the side that ran roughshod over people. Sam had left that side of himself in Dallas and having a reminder was hard to take.

"Aren't you going to need someone to help you run the shop?" he asked Shelly.

"You all forget that I used to run it all by myself. I'll just tell folks we're out of food for a day. After all, we don't even have a menu, right?"

"Yep, that's right," Dave said.

"I don't know." Sam's worry was for himself.

"Come on, Sam, more hands will make it go more quickly," Allie said.

The next day, Shelly put a sign in the window of the Dream Bean stating: "Monday—coffee and muffins only. Gotta go shopping." And in fact, there was some truth to that — she was also looking forward to a quiet day at the Bean.

Monday morning at dawn, Dave, Allie, and Sam hit the highway and headed north to Freeport, while Bo cranked up the *Cassie* and started his own slow journey. In Freeport, Allie had more to pack than she let on, and while most of the boxes fit in the back seat and trunk of Dave's car, the front passenger seat was needed too. That meant Sam would float back to Port Aransas with Allie and Bo.

By the time Bo arrived at the docks, Allie had borrowed a pickup truck from a neighbor and it didn't take but a couple of trips to move her few pieces of furniture to the dock and get them loaded on the deck of the *Cassie*.

"You could have scrubbed it down a little," Allie complained, looking at the deck stained with grease and fish oil and who knew what.

"Oh don't be so picky," Bo said. "I've got tarps and blankets and we'll make sure everything is covered up."

So with Bo barking commands and supervising, the four of them got everything stowed onto the deck with a few more boxes loaded into the corners of the pilothouse. Bo tested all the ropes, grumbling if he found any slack.

By two in the afternoon they were ready to make the voyage back down the coast. "By the time you get there, I'll have the car unloaded and I'll be ready to help you unload the boat," Dave said.

"Thanks sweetie," Allie said, giving him a hug and whispering in his ear, "and use this time alone with Shelly wisely."

He gave her a puzzled look.

"You know what I mean."

"Let's go," Bo growled. "Wind's kicking up a little."

"Bon voyage," Dave said, and then he climbed into his car and drove away. It didn't take long for the rhythm of the highway to clear his mind and allow Allie's parting comment to overtake his thoughts. "Use this time alone with Shelly wisely." It was true that he and Shelly hadn't had any time alone, and now that they'd have some, Dave was nervous. No, he was scared.

Back behind him, the *Cassie* cleared the Coast Guard station and made the turn out into the open water. Bo could see the clouds gathering in the distance but he'd seen it all before and didn't give it any thought. Sam and Allie were keeping their eyes on the cargo and making sure everything was riding well.

The churning sound of the motor worked on Allie and she leaned her back against her mattress and soon fell asleep.

"Good for her," Bo said. "Shelly's been working her real hard lately."

"So how do you feel about Allie coming to live in Port Aransas?" Sam asked.

"It's okay."

Sam was more upbeat. "I think it's great. It's good for her to be near family."

Bo harrumphed.

"What? Did I say something wrong?" Sam asked.

"You all keep talking about 'family,' but you need to be mindful that you aren't Allie's family, and she ain't yours. Friends is all you are. And you're damn sure not her father."

Sam frowned. "I never said I was." He paused, hesitating to say what he wanted to say next, and then he came out and said it. "You need to start acting like you are her father and not just her friend."

Bo took his hand off the wheel and turned to face Sam, lifting his shoulders to make sure Sam knew who was the bigger man. "It's none of your business how I treat my daughter. And what do you know about any of this? Some kind of mystery man who's either giving everyone advice or running away. What's with that, anyway?"

Sam wished he'd kept his mouth shut, and he tried to end the conversation with, "You don't need to know," but Bo pressed further. "I need to know something about you so I can at least know how to talk to you."

There was a long pause. Bo turned back to the controls, looked out the window, and nudged the *Cassie* back on course.

"I hurt a girl. It was an accident." Sam paused a moment. "There's a father in Tennessee who no longer has what you have."

Bo didn't answer, but he was listening. He looked out the window at Allie. He looked out at his daughter.

~ ~ ~ ~ ~

Dave arrived back in Port Aransas at four o'clock, unloaded his car at Allie's rented bungalow, and then went to the Dream Bean where he found Shelly sitting on the deck.

"What's up?"

"That." Shelly pointed to the horizon. Dave climbed up the steps and looked out past the rooftops where deep gray clouds were gathering over the Gulf.

"I'm not liking this," Shelly said. "I hope they're well on their way by now."

"Bo's a good sailor . . . or at least he says he is. Let's give them time before we panic," Dave said. "Besides, I've been looking forward to this time alone with you."

"Oh really," Shelly said, faking surprise. "Whatcha got in mind?"

"How about a walk? We can watch for the *Cassie* from the beach."

"Sure."

Shelly locked the door and they stepped down the plank steps and onto the pavement. A few moments later they were on the beach, where Dave followed Shelly's lead and pulled off his shoes and socks, set them on a bench, and ran toward the throbbing water. The sand was warm, and when the chilly surf washed over Shelly's toes, she shrieked. Dave stood back.

"Chicken," she said, and taunted him with clucks.

"Oh stop it," Dave said, but when he continued to hesitate, Shelly lurched at him and pulled him by the hand into the water. The surprise of it caught Dave off guard and he lost his balance and tumbled face down into the shallow foam, and when he tried to jump up he slipped again and ended up on his back. Completely soaked now, he didn't try to get up but instead reached out for Shelly and grabbed her by the ankle.

"You're coming in too." She kicked at him and landed a glancing blow on his chest, which forced him to let go. "What was that for?"

"Oh no, I didn't mean to," she said and started to lean down and check the damage, but he took another swipe at her and she stepped backward onto the sand.

"You're not going to help me?" he asked.

"I don't trust you."

"I'm the one who should be complaining about trust," he said. "Please." Dave held out a hand and this time she took it and with a groan pulled him up onto his feet. "I suggested a walk, not a swim," he said.

"Then let's walk."

Dave squirmed like a wet dog, trying to shake the cold water out of his clothing and off his skin. With both hands he combed back his soggy hair and then shook down his arms and shivered in the cool evening breeze.

"Maybe we should get you home and into some dry clothes," Shelly said.

"Naw, the wind is chilly but it'll dry me out. Let's go."

With Shelly on the seaside to shield the wind, they walked southward at a slow pace. On the sand in front of them gulls picked at the seaweed and garbage that had washed up on the beach, while a few cars and pickups cruised the drive, kicking up soft plumes of brown sand. As they walked in silence, the warm rays from the slowly setting sun pulled the dampness out of Dave's shirt and he shook back another shiver.

"You okay?" Shelly asked.

"Uh huh," Dave said, but he really wasn't. He was right where he wanted to be at that moment, alone on the beach with Shelly, but a piece of him was three hundred miles and twenty years away back in Dallas. Ever since making the decision to move to Port Aransas, he had managed to keep the past where it belonged, but the closer he got to Shelly, the more the past seemed to come creeping back into view. He knew it to be the birthing pains of letting go and moving on, complete now with a soaking in a sort of amniotic fluid. And at this moment, as he tried to take the first breaths of a new life, he was like a newborn that didn't know how to speak.

Shelly sensed Dave was troubled and she reached out for his hand and stopped him from walking.

"No pressure. No need to hurry. This doesn't need to be anything more than friends walking on the beach."

"I want . . . I want it to be more . . . but . . ."

"There's no rush," she said again, and gently placed her hand on the side of his face. He reached up and patted her fingers, and then brought her hand down to his side and started walking again, this time with their fingers interlocked. For Dave, this had always been the most intimate touch between a man and a woman. It was love, sex, friendship, desire, camaraderie, lust, and respect all rolled into one. In a new relationship it was a first move toward other forms of intimacy but without all the worries about performance and awkwardness and shyness. It was simple. It was pure.

Shelly's feelings were much the same, but this time it felt very different. She had boyfriends in school and dates as an adult, but she had never felt this close to a man before. She had never wanted to be with someone so much and yet felt so safe and content to just hold hands.

They continued to walk for another half hour until the sun rested just on top of the dunes. They knew it was time to turn back toward the Dream Bean, and when they wheeled around they stood still, frozen by the wall of black clouds that had formed while their backs had been turned.

Chapter 30

Sam tapped Allie on the shoulder. "Better come inside."

Allie awoke just in time to feel the *Cassie* rise sharply in the choppy water and then fall hard. "Whoa," she said, sitting up and looking out to see the blackening sky. Sam held out a hand and pulled her to her feet, and she followed him into the pilothouse.

"Everything okay?" she asked.

"I'm afraid your furniture is gonna get a little wet," Bo said.

"Except for the mattress, which needs to be replaced anyway, the rest will hold up. This was all Mom's stuff. It's weathered a few storms."

Bo had noticed the bed frame, chest, and other pieces of vintage ranch oak. They looked familiar to him, but then he wasn't so sure. There was a lot he hadn't paid much attention to back then.

One-by-one, large raindrops began to paint the wood a darker shade, and Bo knew that it was more than the furniture that was in danger, but he kept that to himself. From somewhere deep in his past an old memory from childhood found its way to light and he etched a cross on his chest. And just as if the gesture had been rehearsed and cued, the *Cassie* began to heave and pitch, and the large flat raindrops sharpened and multiplied into a heavy spray that blew horizontally and coated everything, including the windows.

"How can you see anything?" Allie asked.

"I can't," Bo said.

"Then how will you know where we are?"

"By compass and the shape of the shoreline."

Allie looked out the starboard window and couldn't see the shoreline. She couldn't see anything at all. She looked at Sam. He shrugged but didn't say anything. Bo saw them out of the corner of his eye.

"What, you don't trust me? I know the Gulf coast of Texas like the back of my . . ."

"Hand?" Allie said.

"No, I was going to say head."

Allie and Sam both leaned back and looked at the back of Bo's lumpy, bald head.

"Uh . . . okay?" Sam said.

"I know it by feel," Bo explained.

Just then, the bow of the *Cassie* descended and then rose high above them, causing all three of them to fall backwards onto the floor. Allie and Sam scrambled back to their feet but heard a moan and turned to see Bo was still down and wasn't moving. Allie knelt down and found him unconscious with blood oozing from a gash on the back of his head.

"He's hurt," she shouted over the growing roar of the storm and the whine of the engine.

"How bad?" Sam said, his hands on the wheel, straining to see out the window.

"Can't tell, but he's out cold, and he's not going to be piloting anymore."

Allie looked around and out of one of her own boxes she pulled a flannel shirt and lay Bo's head on it, hoping the weight of his head in her lap would stop the bleeding.

"What can I do to help?" Sam shouted.

"You stay at the wheel and try to keep us off the shore. I'll take care of Bo."

Sam shuddered. He didn't know what to do. The view out the window was nothing but shapeless gray. "This is impossible. I can't do this."

"Yes you can. You have to," Allie shouted.

Bo moaned.

"Daddy!" It was the first time Allie had not called Bo by his name.

Coming out of his own gray fog, Bo heard Sam's voice. He raised a hand and pointed toward the *Cassie*'s port side.

"Look," Allie shouted.

Sam looked over his shoulder at Bo and followed the aim of his finger.

"What does it mean?" Allie asked.

Sam rubbed his bristled chin a moment. Gazing out the rain-streaked window and into the darkness, he could see nothing, but then a vision formed in his head of the curve of the Texas coastline—a curve he'd seen on maps taped to the walls of every gas station and trinket shop in Port Aransas.

"He's telling us to steer left, away from the shore. That'll keep us from grounding."

Sam turned the wheel a few degrees to the port, and then without being told, he throttled the engine down to a soft purr. He knew that if they ran out of gas they'd likely drift back into the shore anyway and they'd be beached, or worse, dashed into pieces.

~ ~ ~ ~ ~

By the time the storm rolled down the coast into Port Aransas, Dave and Shelly knew the *Cassie* and its passengers were in trouble. They drove in Shelly's Beetle to the sheriff's office and reported the boat missing, but the storm had blown up so fast that the department was caught off guard, too.

"Folks, not even we can go out in this," the sheriff said. "We're shorthanded and it's too dangerous. We'll go out as soon as it calms down a little. Where did you say they were coming from?"

"Freeport."

"Do you know if they were sailing back on the Gulf or the Intercoastal Waterway?"

Dave looked at Shelly and she shrugged. "We don't know," Dave answered. "Bo never mentioned his route."

But then Shelly remembered. "When he left this morning he went out through the channel into the Gulf."

"Then we'll assume he was coming back the same way. Which means . . ." The sheriff didn't finish the sentence, but Dave and Shelly knew what he was thinking: The *Cassie* was in danger out in the open water.

"Okay, they'll be running past Brazoria, Matagorda, and Calhoun counties." The sheriff shouted across the room to a deputy who was monitoring the storm on a computer. "Hey, Joey, get on the line to the departments up there and let them know we have a missing boat. What's she called?"

"The *Cassie*," Shelly said.

"It's the *Cassie*. Ask them to check their shorelines. We'll do the same down here."

~ ~ ~ ~ ~

Out on the Gulf, the *Cassie* bucked and bobbed into the night, with Sam holding the wheel steady and scanning the darkness for anything that might give cause for hope—or warning of disaster. He'd read about amateur airplane pilots who get disoriented in a dark fog, lose their sense of up and down, and fly their plane into the ground. He knew the same thing might happen with a boat pilot who lost a sense of right or left, so he nudged the wheel to the left every now and then, remembering the direction that Bo had pointed with his thick leathery finger.

Behind him on the floor, Allie tended to her father. The gash in his head had quit bleeding, and now he was conscious but still groggy. When he first came around, he tried to sit up but Allie held his shoulders back.

"Who's at the wheel?" he asked.

"It's Sam," she said.

"How's he doing?"

"Great, as well as you . . . maybe better."

Bo put his head back down and closed his eyes. "Good man," he said.

The storm was coming and going in waves now, but visibility was still minimal and they puttered along not knowing if they were still following the shoreline or headed deep into the Gulf. Sam was contemplating stepping out onto the deck with hopes of seeing something when the pilothouse was filled with a bright light and the ear-piercing blare of a ship's horn. Seeing the bow of a tanker coming straight at them, Sam spun the wheel, kicking the *Cassie*'s bow to the starboard, and the two boats were now running parallel to each other in opposite directions. But they still weren't clear and the *Cassie* shrieked and shuddered as she skidded a thousand feet down the steel hull of the massive tanker.

Just as the two boats cleared and the grinding ended, the *Cassie* began to jump and bounce in the tanker's wake, leaning hard to starboard and then to port. Sam tried to turn the wheel to flatten her out and that just made it worse.

"Turn her toward port and ride between the swells," Bo croaked. Sam did as he was told and the *Cassie* calmed down and was back to fighting just the storm.

~ ~ ~ ~ ~

Shelly and Dave leaned against each other on a bench, fading in and out of sleep, when the phone rang. They heard a conversation and then the hurried footsteps of the sheriff.

"Good news: The *Cassie* was seen by a tanker off of Matagorda Island. Almost ran her over, but the captain said they cleared and last he saw the *Cassie* was afloat."

"They're okay!" Shelly sat up straight on the bench.

"They're still out there in the storm, but we know where to look now," the sheriff said. "Why don't you two go home and get some rest? We'll call you when we know something."

Shelly gave him her cell number and she started to drive herself and Dave back to the Dream Bean, but then Shelly turned away at the last minute. "We're going home," she said.

At her house, Shelly walked into the kitchen and started filling a glass decanter with water.

"What are you doing?" Dave asked.

"Making coffee."

"Why didn't we go on to the Bean if you wanted to do that? I thought we came here to rest."

Shelly dumped the water into the sink, set the

decanter down, and stood quietly for a moment. Dave was right. She was running on adrenaline-fueled autopilot and not making any sense. She took a deep breath and lowered her shoulders, and the next thing she knew Dave was wrapping his arms around her from behind. She slowly turned and their eyes met. Dave looked like he wanted to speak, and Shelly repeated what she had said on the beach: "No hurry, no pressure."

But Dave wasn't feeling pressure now. The past no longer nipped at his heels. He felt free for the first time, and the first thing he did with his freedom was to draw Shelly tightly into his arms and kiss her.

~ ~ ~ ~ ~

Sam stared out the window of the *Cassie* in a sort of stupor, his senses dulled by the endless roar of the driving rain and the rising and falling of the boat that was sometimes smooth and rhythmic and sometimes jarring to the bone. The storm had gone on for so long that Sam had lost all measure of time. He'd gripped the wheel so hard that his hands were numb. In this suspension of time and feeling his only clear thought was to wonder whether he'd ever see the sunlight again, or the dry land, or Shelly and Dave, or anyone or anything else that he'd grown to care about. He wasn't scared and he wasn't worried. He was just worn and tired and sad that maybe this is where his story would end. He knew that at any moment a wave might turn them upside down, or a shattering crash would be all he would know of the *Cassie* being dashed against the shoreline.

He was imagining what that fraction of a second might feel like when a murmur brought him back into the moment, and he looked over his shoulder and remembered that he was not alone. Allie and Bo were still with him, and as he watched the daughter doting on her father, a warm wave of contentment washed over him. At least these two had discovered the unique bonds of true family, and he was grateful for that.

Sam turned back to face the darkness outside and realized that the roar of the storm in his head was gone and there was now a ringing in his ears, the type you get when the brain tries to replace a persistent loud noise with something new. And then through the ringing he began to hear the sound of the engine, which he had felt but not heard since the storm began. He became aware that the windows were no longer coated with a watery film but were speckled as the rain slowed from a torrent to a shower to a sprinkle. The outline of the bow became visible as the thick blanket of clouds was torn into long narrow strips through which the light from a half moon brought depth and shape to the boat and the surface of the water.

With the sea no longer pitching, Allie left her father's side, opened the door, and leaned out to look toward the bow and stern. The moonlight revealed what they all had suspected but had dared not talk about: The deck was bare. Somewhere in the storm the furniture had torn loose from its tie downs and had been washed away.

Allie sighed, and Bo, who was awake but laying on the floor with a duffle for a pillow, asked, "What is it, dear?"

"We lost our load."

"I'm so sorry. This weren't such a good idea."

Allie knelt down beside her father and patted his shoulder. "It'll be good to start fresh in a new town with new stuff."

With the rain no longer impairing his vision, Sam scanned the horizon and saw the faint twinkle of lights out ahead and on the starboard side. "That's a relief," he said.

"What do you see?" Bo asked.

"Lights . . . which means we didn't drift so far out into the Gulf."

"Is one of the lights taller than the others?"

"Yes, and much brighter."

"That's Lydia Ann . . . the lighthouse. She'll guide us home. Just angle in toward her now but go past her a ways and then watch for the jetties. Turn starboard between 'em and you'll enter the channel."

Bo squeezed Allie's hand. "We're almost home."

Chapter 31

"Look, there's the *Cassie*!"

"I knew the old salt could bring her in."

"That Bo's one of a kind for sure."

Word had spread through Port Aransas that the *Cassie* had been caught in the storm, and when the news came around that she'd been sighted and was on her way home, the townspeople crowded the shorelines from the beach on into the channel.

Shelly and Dave got the news too, with a phone call that almost knocked Dave off the sofa where he was sleeping. Shelly came running from the bedroom, sleepy and dazed, and almost shrieked when she saw Dave sprawled on the sofa. For a moment she had forgotten he was there but then her head cleared and she remembered what had happened. She looked down at herself and was relieved to find she was still fully clothed, as he was, and then she worried that her hair was a mess but the phone rang loudly again.

"Sorry, I must've dumped my phone here when we got in." Shelly picked up her cell phone from the table beside the sofa and answered. It was the sheriff. The

Coast Guard had launched a boat and intercepted the *Cassie* ten miles north of the lighthouse. She was damaged but coming in under her own power. And there was one injured man on board but nothing too serious.

"Poor Sam. He said he didn't want to go. We shouldn't have pushed him," Shelly said.

"I'm sure it's just some bumps and bruises," Dave reassured.

Shelly and Dave made the short drive to the Dream Bean, where a crowd was already gathered on the porch, looking out past the boats and buildings for the first glimpse of the *Cassie* in the cove.

"Give us a moment to set up." Shelly and Dave pushed through the crowd and unlocked the door.

"Better get all the pots going," Dave said. "Do we have enough change in the till?"

"We're not keeping count this morning." Shelly walked to the back and came out with the galvanized bucket that had served as a tip jar on Christmas Eve.

The aroma of coffee wafted through the shop and out the front door, drawing some people inside. Dave passed out cups and lids to those who lined up at the two carafes while Shelly started brewing more. As she expected, dollar bills and coins began to fill the bucket.

Shelly was daydreaming about the past few hours with Dave when a shout rang from the porch: "There she is," and just like that the Dream Bean was empty.

"Aren't you coming?" Dave asked.

"I don't know, maybe I should wait here . . ."

"Don't be stupid." Dave grabbed Shelly by the hand and pulled her out the door.

By the time they got down to the docks, the *Cassie* was turning into Turtle Cove and coming toward the docks with a small flotilla following her. She was listing to the starboard, with her portside gunwale broken, her steel hull dented from the brush with the tanker. Her stern deck was completely bare.

The crowd followed the *Cassie* all the way into the slip where a couple of men jumped on board to tie her down as the engine was cut off from inside. There was silence on the pier with everyone waiting to cheer when Bo stepped out of the pilothouse, and then a collective gasp when Sam stepped out instead.

"We need a doctor," Sam shouted hoarsely. An ambulance that had been parked nearby during the search rolled up as close as it could and paramedics pushed their way on board with a gurney. A few moments later they walked Bo out of the pilothouse, and a cheer went up when he saw the gurney and began to object loudly.

"Aw, he's okay," someone shouted, and a chuckle rolled through the crowd.

With Allie's insistence, Bo sat down and then laid back on the gurney. The paramedics strapped him down and rolled him across the creaky planks to the ambulance. Inside, Bo gave the order, "No damn sirens or I'm gonna jump out of here," and the ambulance rolled away quietly.

Sam was the last person off the boat and was surrounded by people asking for details of what had happened. "There's nothing to tell," he said.

"But you saved them?" someone pressed.

"No . . . Bo did the saving. I just did what he told me. He's a smart man. He knows what he's doing out there."

Sam looked through the crowd and when he saw Shelly and Dave he mouthed the word "please." They stepped up and with one of them on either side they escorted him to the Dream Bean and up the steps.

"Let's get you some hot food," Shelly said.

Sam saw the people crowded into the Dream Bean. "I really just want to go home," and then he said aloud what he had mouthed a moment earlier: "please."

"Then at least let me drive you," Dave said. Sam nodded.

As they drove down the highway in silence, Dave glanced over at Sam and saw him staring blankly out the window. It reminded him of that first day when he and Sam met on the beach and they drove in silence to the Dream Bean. The big difference now was that he knew something of the heart and soul of this bedraggled beach dweller, and what he knew made him proud for their friendship.

Dave pulled through the gate of the trailer park.

"Thanks, I'll see you later," Sam said as he climbed out of the car. Dave waited to make sure he got inside the trailer okay, and then he drove back into town and to the clinic to check on Bo and Allie.

Inside the trailer, Sam started to unbutton his shirt, which was stiff and rough from the dried salt water, but he was too tired to continue and climbed into bed. A light breeze rocked the trailer and soon he was sound asleep.

Back in town, a doctor stitched up the back of Bo's head and told him he had a concussion. He'd be okay, but they'd hold him for a day or two just to be safe. The prognosis for the *Cassie* was not so good. Other captains who checked her out said she would need major repairs if she were ever to be allowed back out on the water. It was a miracle she'd made it home and wasn't at the bottom of the Gulf.

As for Allie, her clothing and jewelry, mementos and personal items had traveled safely in Dave's car, but her furniture was at the bottom of the Gulf. She was disappointed but philosophical. She still had her life and her family, her father, especially, and she had Sam to thank for that.

But Allie was not without possessions for long. The money collected in the bucket on Shelly's counter was given to her to help buy household goods. Dream Bean regulars dug into their garages and sheds and gathered a bed and enough loose furniture to get Allie started in her new bungalow. When a second bed showed up at her front door, Allie set it up in a small extra room for Bo.

"Live on dry land like one of you rats? Never," Bo said from his hospital room.

But Allie proved she was her father's daughter and pushed back hard. "You're not going back on that rusty old boat. I don't care if Mom's name is on the back, I'll put holes in it and sink it for sure if you even try to go back there and live."

Bo was stumped. He really did just want to go home, as beat up as it was, but he was beginning to like the doting of this headstrong girl. He rubbed his bald head for a moment and then made a counteroffer.

"Okay, I'll bunk with you at night, but only if you'll let me work on the boat during the day."

Allie hesitated.

"The *Cassie's* not going to fix herself, and she's all I got."

"All you've got?"

"I mean for making a living."

"Wow, I'm really feeling the love."

Bo thought about what Sam said on the boat—about being a father. He took Allie by the hand and then put both his hands on her shoulders.

"Listen, kiddo, my life hasn't been the same since we found each other, and I don't want any of that to change. But that boat means more to me than just your momma's name on the stern. That boat has been my home and my life for twenty-five years. I need to keep that connection too."

With Bo standing so close, Allie wrapped her arms around his barrel waist and hugged him tightly until she heard him gasp a little.

"Okay Bo. Okay Daddy."

~ ~ ~ ~ ~

Sam hit the floor hard. For a moment, as he lay on his back, the trailer looked every bit like the pilothouse of the *Cassie*. He'd been dreaming that he was still out on the water, riding the storm with Allie and Bo, and a stiff wind hit the trailer at the precise moment that the *Cassie* plunged sideways into another trough. Only this time the boat had turned over and Sam was flailing in the cold water. And it was that flailing that sent Sam tumbling out of his bed and onto the floor.

Sam lay still for a moment as his eyes focused and his other senses sharpened. Then he sat up and felt a pain in his arm. He rolled up his shirt sleeve to find a large knot growing on his elbow. How ironic, he thought, to have escaped death and injury on the Gulf and then get hurt falling out of bed. He stood up and went to the sink to wash his face. Looking at the clock, he saw that it was early afternoon. He wasn't expected at the market, and he figured Shelly and Dave could get along without him, so he changed into clean shorts and a loose short sleeve shirt and walked down to the beach.

Looking out across the water, Sam saw a fishing boat and a pair of tankers shimmering in the sun. In the past, the vessels had looked like bathtub toys, but now he was keenly aware that there were people out there who might be in danger with a sudden shift of the wind. And, he had new respect for all the men out there like Bo who knew the Gulf like the "back of their head."

In town, Bo was fast asleep in his hospital bed, with Allie snoozing in a chair close by. Dave and Shelly had gone back to their respective homes and they too were catching some much-needed sleep. But Shelly was restless and after an hour or so she went back to the Dream Bean. She was surprised—but pleased—to find Dave sitting on the porch.

"You too?" he asked.

"Me too what?" She blushed and then quickly hopped up the steps to unlock the front door. Dave followed her inside.

"Couldn't unwind?" he asked.

"Oh . . . that." Her voice fell.

"You sound disappointed."

"No . . . I just figured I could use the time to get a few things done here. After the excitement this morning, nobody's gonna come around this afternoon. They'll be back tomorrow, of course. So, how long were you sitting on the porch?"

"Just a little while. You know . . . it might be good for business if someone else had a key."

Shelly smirked. "That's a great idea, Dave. I'll go down to the hardware store this afternoon and get a copy made for Allie." She tried to keep a straight face but when she saw Dave stick out his tongue like a petulant six-year-old, she snickered. "Okay, okay, yes, I'll get keys made for you and Allie both."

Dave stepped behind the counter and started looking for things to do, but as he watched Shelly going about her business, moving lightly and happily and humming to herself, his heartbeat quickened, his lungs wouldn't expand and he felt like he would faint. He waited until Shelly came close, and then he took her in his arms and spun her out of sight behind the wall where he searched deeply and found the sweet breath of life.

Chapter 32

When Sam entered the market the next morning he was greeted with pats on the back and handshakes.

"You da man," said Marty, and he put his hand up for a high-five but lowered it for a more subtle knuckle bump when Sam hesitated. Sam grinned sheepishly and then walked to the break room to punch his time card and start his shift. When he came back out into the store and walked up to the front, he was startled by the sharp sound of applause coming from the other employees and customers who were waiting for him.

In the center of the crowd was Maggie Gifford, who reached over and pulled Sam to her side.

"Sam, we're all so proud of you and, well, it's rare that we would ever do this in the middle of a month, but Lucy has agreed to share her spot on the wall with you."

She pointed to the wall: beside Lucy's "Employee of the Month" photo was a photo of Sam taken from his employment application. His hair was windblown and wild, his expression unsettled; it was a fitting representation of the man who had emerged as a hero from Bo's boat just twenty-four hours earlier.

"And Sam, your reign will continue into next month," Maggie said.

There was more applause and several calls for "speech," but when everyone quieted down, all Sam could manage was a hoarse, "Thank you." It was the first words he had spoken since Dave had driven him home the day before, and even Sam was surprised at how much the stress and strain of the storm had impaired him. So he waved at the crowd and mouthed another thank you, and everyone dispersed.

Sam tried to work quietly through his shift, but every time he turned a corner and encountered someone new, he received a back slap or handshake or hug. He had become comfortable with it until an elderly woman practically pinned him against the frozen food case.

"Sam, you done well; we're so proud of you." And then she took his hand and said: "You're one of us. You belong." She patted his hand and shuffled away.

The statement burrowed into Sam's head and down deep into his soul. He shivered for a moment, and it had nothing to do with the frozen food case he was leaning against. Back in Dallas he had known transplants from other cities who had never felt completely at home, who described a feeling of still being a visitor even though they had left "home" years earlier. Sam had known that feeling these past two years on the island—of being a visitor who might someday go home again—but now he was being told he was, in fact, home. Tears welled up in his eyes, a combination of gratitude for having been accepted, and grief over the loss of who he had been. He turned and looked at his reflection in the glass door and didn't recognize the man he saw.

That evening Sam walked back down the highway to the trailer knowing that the world had changed. He was no longer anonymous. He would no longer be given the leeway afforded to a guest—even a perpetual guest. He could no longer come and go as he wished. He could no longer just walk away from something that was uncomfortable. Now there would be expectations and responsibilities.

That night as he lay in bed, with Miles Davis playing softly on the phonograph, Sam felt the tug of unfinished business. As long as he was a guest in Port Aransas, there was always the possibility that he might go back to Dallas and tidy things up. It was mostly a mind game that he played with himself, but now that Port Aransas was home, he could no longer pretend that things could wait.

The next morning he got up early and walked into town with purpose, knowing what he must do. His first stop was at the market, where he found Maggie Gifford in the office.

"I was wondering if I could have a couple of days off?"

"This is rather sudden," she said, looking at the schedule. "I suppose if Marty doesn't mind covering for you, then we can make it work."

"Tell him I'll match his pay," Sam said.

"We'll see what he says."

"I'll match his pay . . . or anyone else's. I've gotta go." And he was out the door.

His next stop was the Dream Bean, where he startled Shelly as he thrust open the door and rattled the bells against the glass.

"Good grief. You're getting as bad as Bo, bursting in here like that." She caught her breath. "But it's good to see you."

"You too. Is Dave in yet?"

"No, but he will be soon."

Sam hesitated. "I was wondering if I could have a few days off?"

"I don't see why not. Is there something we can help you with?"

"Oh . . . no, I just need a few days to take care of some things."

Dave walked in just then and Sam didn't give him a chance to say good morning.

"Dave, I was wondering if I could borrow your car for a few days?"

"Uh . . . I don't . . . you do know how to drive, right?"

"Oh sure, I just haven't needed to since I've been here."

Dave's keys were still in his hand and he fumbled with them as he considered Sam's request and the urgency in his voice. It was as if he was speaking to a different man.

Dave glanced at Shelly and then probed Sam further. "Is there some place I can take you?"

"No, I need to go by myself."

"Where is that?"

"I can't tell you."

Dave looked at Shelly again. She nodded at him, and he continued.

"Well, Sam, I really don't care where you need to go, but I think I have a right to know where my car is going?"

Sam was in a corner, and he knew it. He tapped his hand against his leg for a moment, and then he told what he could.

"I need to go to Dallas."

By now Shelly was standing next to Dave, and she was ready with the next line of questioning.

"Okay, Sam . . . spill. What's this about?"

"I just . . . I just need to take care of a few things. It will just take a couple of days."

"Business back home?" Shelly asked.

Sam looked them both sharply in the eye. "No . . . business in Dallas. Port A is my home."

Allie came in about that time and when she heard what was up, she pulled her small wad of keys out of her purse, unhooked her car key and pushed it into Sam's hand. "Here ya go. It's all yours." She stuck her tongue out at Dave and then said to Sam, "It's no yuppy Beamer but it'll get you there."

Sam looked at the key a moment, stunned by Allie's unquestioning trust.

"It's parked in the alley. Needs some gas—and probably a quart of oil—but it's ready when you want it."

"Thank you."

Allie patted his shoulder and walked to the back to put on an apron and get ready for the morning rush.

Leaving the others to wonder about his mission, Sam walked out the front door and around the corner where Allie's Toyota was parked. Looking in the window—and pausing when he saw his reflection again—he opened the door slowly and sat down in the driver's seat. He rubbed the steering wheel, getting used to the feel of it. Then he put the key into the ignition and turned it. The vibration coming up through the floorboard and the steering column reminded him of that first time he cranked up his parent's car as a freshly licensed driver. His errand on that evening had been a quick run to the grocery store for his mother, but in his own mind it had been a journey as grand as Lindbergh flying across the Atlantic Ocean for the first time.

Sam carefully shifted the car into drive and then took his foot off the brake and slowly rolled forward. Fully aware that he was unlicensed, he moved carefully and deliberately out of the alley and onto the street, signaling every turn like a dutiful drivers-ed teacher. When he got out onto the highway, he watched his speed carefully and made a wide, slow turn into the trailer park.

Getting out and walking up to his door, Sam looked back at Allie's car, both afraid and excited about what the next couple of days might have in store. Inside the trailer, he folded and packed a couple of changes of clothes into a shopping bag that would have to do for luggage. In the little bathroom that was no bigger than a closet he gathered his toothbrush, razor, soap, and comb, and dropped them into a well-used ziplock bag. He dropped the whole bundle onto the floor of the car behind the passenger seat and then he was ready to go.

As he backed up to drive away, he stopped to look at the trailer for a moment. This was home, he thought. And then he said it aloud to himself. He didn't want to forget that no matter what happened in Dallas, he would come back to this place . . . to this home.

Sam drove back through town past the market and Sea Siren and made the turn to the ferry landing. As he waited in the line of cars that were making the crossing to go to jobs in Rockport and beyond, he realized that he had never given any thought to making that crossing again. He'd been in a kind of limbo where he hadn't given any thought to the future.

With the arrival of the next two ferries, the cars moved forward, and when it was his turn to board Sam found himself looking across the channel from the front row. He watched as the workers raised and chained the metal ramp that also served as a barrier, and then without his immediately noticing the ferry with its load of vehicles began floating forward. It was so much different from the voyage he had taken just two days earlier. So smooth and so pleasant that he was disappointed when it ended so quickly.

But it did, and as the ramp lowered again and the flagman signaled for Sam to roll off, he did something else that he hadn't done in two years: he prayed. For safe travel—in the literal sense that he didn't want to encounter any dangers or problems on the highway. And certainly he wanted to return safely to Port Aransas with Allie's car. But more than that, he prayed over those two things he needed to take care of. He could not predict how they would go, but good or bad, he had to do them. If Port Aransas was to be home, he had to confirm for himself that Dallas no longer was home. And, equally important, he had to lay down a burden he still was carrying.

Chapter 33

Dave wasn't expecting a knock at his door, and when he opened it he was surprised to find Shelly there, and when he saw the expression on her face he turned away to wipe the tears from his eyes.

"Come in," he mumbled, keeping his back to her as she walked past him into the little front room. Just a moment earlier he was stomping around the house, shouting angrily at the top of his lungs, unable to find the beginning or end of his emotions. And he was confused because he wasn't sure what had set him off. He'd had a good day with Shelly and Allie at the Dream Bean, and after they closed down the kitchen he'd come home for a while to clean up and rest. And he'd done all of that but then something snapped. He wondered how long Shelly had been outside and if she had heard his angry rant at God and the doctors and the universe for allowing Debby to suffer so badly.

"Not fair!" He had shouted into the ceiling as if his words might break through the drywall and the roof above and make their way to some cosmic listener who might care. But at that moment he felt that nobody was listening—nobody cared or could possibly care. And then he had fallen to his knees, spent and sobbing, when the knock came at the door and broke the spell. Now Dave looked over at Shelly, who was standing in front of the sofa, waiting quietly for him while the television flickered across the room. Dave walked over, picked up the remote and touched the off button, and then motioned for Shelly to sit down on the sofa beside him. It was quiet, and Shelly waited for Dave to speak.

Dave pulled his legs up and rested his feet on the edge of the coffee table. He rubbed his knees a moment, sore from the hardwood floor, and then he spoke.

"These are strange days. I am so perfectly fine and okay—and in fact, in love . . . with you—and yet I am so miserable and have so much contempt for the world and for the universe and for God."

Shelly sat in the corner of the sofa so she could see Dave, but she was silent.

"It's been almost two years, and that should be time enough to heal, but the truth is I don't know if there will be any healing this side of heaven. So . . ." He hesitated.

"What?" Shelly asked.

"I don't think I can be who you want me to be."

"And just who is that?"

"Someone who is stable—without all this baggage."

Shelly laughed out loud. "Are you kidding me? You should look in my garage. I don't have baggage; I have steamer trunks."

Dave smiled at the mental picture, and then his expression turned serious again.

Shelly reached across the space between them and took Dave's hand.

"Listen to me . . . you are the most stable person I know. You really are. But stability doesn't mean you aren't beat up and bruised. If we live long enough we'll all have some baggage. Besides, yours is pretty cool."

"What's that supposed to mean?"

"I mean, for you to have loved someone so much and be shaken by the loss but still want to dive in again . . . that's something a lot of girls would like to get close to."

"Including you?"

"Yes."

Dave pulled Shelly close and buried his face in her hair. They held the embrace for a moment and when he pulled his head away, a few strands of her hair stuck to his tear-dampened cheek.

"Good grief," he said as he untangled himself.

"What now?"

"I'm a mess. Don't know whether to laugh or cry."

"You're allowed to do both, you know."

Dave sighed and reached for the television remote. He was tired of being so open and vulnerable. He just wanted to be quiet for a while. It was evening and the news came on, but he turned the volume down to a whisper. Shelly pulled her feet up onto the table next to Dave's and rested her head on his shoulder. He was calmed by her closeness and wasn't paying any attention to the television when a gust of wind rattled the window and he realized what had set him off. The same thing had happened earlier and he was taken back to the little rent house on Glasgow Street in Dallas where he and Debby had lived cheaply for a year while saving money for something nicer. The house was hot in the summer and cold in the winter and when the winds would blow, the old double-hung windows would rattle in their frames.

The thought of it all made Dave sigh again, and he struggled to push away the successive waves of regret that had overtaken him earlier—the charm of that little house, the squalor of that neighborhood and the burglary that chased them to another rental, the joy of their dream house tempered by busyness that kept them from finishing all the projects they had planned, and finally the illness that came and swept away any chances of creating the life and home that Debby had dreamed of. Dave felt like wailing all over again, but Shelly's soft breathing brought him back to the present, and he made a silent vow that he would not make the mistake again of putting off or holding back.

~ ~ ~ ~ ~

Just down the street, Allie shouted at Bo from the kitchen. "Dinner's ready."

The old sailor rolled out of bed and onto his feet with

a heavy groan, his head throbbing from the lingering effects of the concussion.

Allie shouted again. "Didya hear?"

"Just wait a minute. I'm 'bout half dead in here, in case you forgot."

Allie turned off the burners and carried a covered frying pan and pot to the table. She looked up and saw her father coming slowly down the hallway, pressing the palm of one hand against the wall for support.

"Here, let me help," she said, arriving just in time to offer him a shoulder to lean on as he entered the room.

"You sure you're up to this?" Bo asked. "Might have been better to let me stay on the boat."

"This is exactly why you should *not* be on the boat. Now, sit down here and don't open your mouth unless there's a fork full of food going in."

Bo grumbled as he sat down hard in the chair, which like most everything else in the house was a gift from neighbors and strangers.

"So, what have we got here?" Bo reached to lift the lid off the pot and Allie rapped the lid with a wooden spoon, just missing his hand.

"You wait now. That's hotter than you think." To prove the point she pulled the cup towel off her shoulder and used it to remove one lid and then another. Bo leaned forward to look in and the steam rose up around his bald head.

"Smells good. Looks okay, too."

Allie picked up his plate and loaded it with crusted pork chops, wild rice, and green beans, and set it back down in front of him.

"I bet you'll like it. You've maybe even had the chops before."

"How's that?"

"It's Mom's recipe."

Bo forked up a large portion and shoveled it into his mouth. It might have been scalding hot but Bo didn't flinch. He chewed and swallowed and then he forked up another large bite. Watching him as she cut small pieces for herself, Allie wasn't sure if her father really liked it or was just hungry.

"So . . . is it okay?"

Bo put his fork on the plate, pulled the napkin from the table, and wiped his mouth.

"It's really good. I can't say that I remember it, but I do know that your mother was a good cook so it fits that you are, too."

Allie smiled at Bo's rare compliment. She knew that didn't come naturally to him and that he wouldn't say it if he didn't mean it.

"Glad you like it, and there's plenty . . . so tank up."

Bo dropped his fork and stared at Allie.

"What now?" she asked.

"Where'd you get that . . . 'tank up'?"

"Mom used to say that."

Bo rubbed his brow for a moment, and when he

lowered his hand Allie noticed his eyes were red and watery. She reached across the table and put her hand on top of his. "Tell me."

Bo cleared his throat. "She got that from me, and only because I got it from my grandpa. I haven't heard it in years, because I haven't said it in years."

The statement opened a new door of understanding for Allie. She was eager to know more about her father if he was willing to talk. She moved slowly.

"So . . . there was never anyone else after mother?"

"No, it's just been easier on my own. That doesn't mean I haven't had some lady friends. There's been one or two over the years that I've enjoyed spending time with."

"Ever get serious with any of them?"

"No."

"Why not?"

"Just didn't." Bo was uncomfortable so he turned the questions back on his daughter. "Why are you so interested? I'm the one who should be asking you about boyfriends. Did you leave Freeport to run away from someone, or are you just footloose and fancy free?"

Allie snorted a laugh. "Really, does anyone say that anymore?"

"You know what I'm asking."

"I don't have anyone . . . and I don't need anyone. I guess that makes me just like you, huh?"

"So why didn't you just stay over there?"

The question put Allie on the spot. She couldn't just brush it aside, and yet she didn't have a particularly good answer. She thought about it for a moment. "Just wanted a new start I suppose. Freeport's a refinery town. I've always liked the tourist vibe over here."

They both went back to eating, eager to escape the questions. They were finishing up when the sound of a ship horn out on the water stirred Bo.

"Hey, how about walking down to the pier with me? Everyone's been telling me how beat up the *Cassie* is, but I'd like to see for myself."

"What was it you said before you came in here . . . something about being half dead?"

"Oh you know that was just me talking. Besides, this wonderful meal picked me up."

Allie wasn't so sure.

Bo pushed back from the table. "Come on, the exercise will be good for us both."

Allie gave in. She put the dirty dishes in the sink, and they set out on the quarter-mile walk to the marina. They made small talk on the way with Allie asking Bo what he knew about this house or that shop.

When they got within sight of the *Cassie*, Bo stopped and just stared. The mast was bent to the port at a thirty-degree angle about three quarters of the way up. The net boom and rigging—where Allie's furniture had been tied off—was completely gone, and all the remaining lines and cables were broken and dangling free, some of them rattling against the hull in the evening breeze.

Bo started walking again, and when they got beside her, Allie broke the silence. "Pretty bad, huh?"

Bo didn't answer but held out a hand and helped Allie over the gunwale and onto the deck, and then she did the same for him. He stood for the longest time just looking around, and then he started poking at things with a hand here and a foot there. Several times he pushed hard on the wooden deck with his foot to test its strength, and Allie could see the look on his face when the boards gave too much under his weight. Walking from the stern to the bow, Bo saw that large sections of the gunwale and some of the hull above the water line had been peeled off by the tanker. Bo walked all the way to the bow where a white heron sitting on the prow shrieked loudly and then flapped its large wings and lifted off to an unknown destination.

Bo turned and looked back at the pilothouse and saw that several panes of glass were cracked and one was gone completely. He shuffled back down the starboard side and entered the pilothouse where for the first time he saw the blood stain on the floor. He reached up and felt the bandage on the back of his scalp.

Allie waited outside, and when Bo came back out into the fading glow of sunset she could read the disappointment on his face.

"Wanna sit down a moment?" She pointed to some wooden crates that were stacked on the pier.

Bo sat down, but instead of the crates he tested a section of the remaining gunwale and sat there, resting a hand on each knee.

Allie sat beside him. "What's the verdict, captain?"

"She's a sure-enough disaster." Bo rubbed his forehead as if to squeeze out another opinion, but none came forth.

Allie pressed. "Can she be fixed?"

"I suppose anything can be fixed. But . . . I don't know . . ." His voice trailed off as he retreated into thought.

"What is it, Daddy?"

There was that word again, and this time when Bo heard it he was warmed by it. He put an arm around Allie's back and held her close for a moment. "I'm tired. Let's go back."

Indeed, Bo was tired . . . but not from the walk. Seeing the *Cassie* that way—her bow warped, sides beaten in, rigging gone—he knew that repairing her would take energy and money, both of which he was short on. But more than that, the pilothouse suddenly looked cramped and cold compared to the room at Allie's. And the blood on the floor reminded him of how lucky he was to be walking around. Still, his pride was strong, and he straightened his back and raised his head high to prove to himself he was still tough. But by the time they reached Allie's door he was slumped forward and in pain. He was tired.

Chapter 34

Sam didn't waste any time. He drove up through the heart of Texas without much regard for what was happening in the towns and on the farms that slipped past his windshield. Except for a stop near Waco to refuel, he kept pushing ahead. Behind his eyes, his mind was running through what he might say, what the response might be, and what he might say after that. He wondered if the trip would be a total bust—that perhaps nobody would be home. That led to speculation about whether that might be a sign from a generous and gracious God that his debts had been paid and he should now get on with his life. But that line of thinking led him to wonder: if God did in fact work that way, then what was he to make of the past two years? Had he really just run away to Port Aransas, or had the time on the island been a God-devised "time out"—to get him out of Dallas so the dust could settle and he wouldn't be tempted to do something stupid that would make things worse? And what about the trip in the storm? Was that just by chance and their survival a case of good luck? Or had God raised up the wind and the waves and tossed Bo on his head so that Sam could gain a little courage—like the cowardly lion on the road to Oz?

Sam didn't have any answers and the questions were swept aside by the time he reached the Dallas County line and found himself in rush hour traffic. He was glad to be in Allie's little Toyota because he felt like he had more room to breathe in the crowded highway lanes, until eighteen wheelers pulled up on either side of him and he felt that he might be crushed at any moment. At the place where the interstate highway curved down onto the long bridge across the Trinity River, the heavy traffic began to divide up into those heading east toward Louisiana and north toward Oklahoma, and Sam felt his arms unglue themselves from his sides, as if pulling them in had made him smaller. At the end of the bridge, he took the exit ramp he had taken so many times that carried him out of harm's way and onto the quieting streets of downtown Dallas.

Now he was looking out the car windows deliberately because this was familiar territory, with the tall buildings housing many of the clients he had worked with and their street-level portals opening to the restaurants and bars he had frequented for lunch and happy hour. It all looked familiar to him, but as he looked closer he could see that many of the eateries had been changed out, and he knew the same was probably true in the businesses above. And then he made the turn onto St. Paul Street and saw the glass and steel building where his office had been. He panicked for a moment and looked at the dashboard clock, and then he relaxed his grip on the steering wheel when he saw that it was 6:30 and realized there would be nobody left on the street who might recognize him. As he drove by, he stole a quick glance into the glass lobby and saw nobody but a security guard at a granite desk and a maintenance man buffing the floors.

Sam rolled out the north side of downtown into the growing forest of high-rise condos and apartments that were not standing two years earlier, and then into the more familiar environs of Turtle Creek Boulevard and its namesake stream just to the right. And then Sam's face flushed hot as he realized what he had done—he had driven himself right back to where he had been on that night when everything had gone wrong. Before he could change his course and turn down a side street he was face-to-face with the giant oak tree where he had crashed his car. As his eyes fixed on it, it seemed to stare back at him like a brooding demon in the fading light. And then Sam felt the wheels of the car brush the curb and he pulled the steering wheel to the left, regained control, and continued down the boulevard another hundred yards or so until he found a place where he could pull over. He got out of the car and ran down the grassy slope to the creek side, feeling like he would vomit. But it wasn't his stomach that was upset; it was his soul. And instead of hanging his head and losing what little he had eaten that day, he raised his face to the sky and let out a wail that rose up into the oaks and pecans and sent mockingbirds and doves fluttering from their roosts.

And then all was quiet again except for the sounds of the city in the deepening dusk—the traffic streaming in small waves down the boulevard, music wafting faintly from a rooftop bar, a pair of joggers crunching their shoes down the sidewalk, the shuffle of birds reclaiming their overnight nests. Sam looked back up the curving boulevard with the oak tree silhouetted against the towers of downtown in the background. In that moment, the questions he had posed on the highway came back to him. Had he been so absent-minded as to just stumble back into this pain by chance? Or had God distracted him and brought him back to this place to rub his nose in his sin once more? And then from somewhere inside he didn't so much hear the answers as feel a wave of release that he knew to be an answer just the same. He had come to Dallas with a burden to lay down, and he hadn't planned the when or the how of it, but it had happened just now and he was at peace. As important, he had come to confirm that Dallas was no longer his home, and the way was clear to do that now. It wouldn't be easy, but now he had the courage to face it.

Sam got back in the car, this time with his senses fully engaged, and in a short time he made the turn onto the street where he once dreamed of being a king. It all looked so familiar to him, and for a fraction of a second he sensed that he could just roll down the street, into the driveway, and walk into the house. But as he came to the familiar bend of the road and saw the large live oak tree that spread gracefully over the lawn, he was jolted back to reality and he pulled over to the curb. The confidence and determination that had carried him more than three hundred miles from the coast was suddenly thin and fragile. He lowered his head so he wouldn't be recognized. But more than that, to take a deep breath. And then when he was ready, he rolled forward the rest of the way and pulled to a stop in front of the house. Getting out, he noted the well-groomed lawn that he had paid to have planted but never took the time to enjoy. He rang the doorbell and then took a step backward off the small porch. His heart began to pound as he heard footsteps, and he sucked in a large breath as he saw movement through the beveled glass windows framing the heavy mahogany door. And then the door opened and he saw her.

"Yes?" she asked.

Sam stood silently and waited for Brenda to recognize him, but she didn't. She saw a man with wild, sun-bleached hair. Sunburned skin. A loose, casual shirt, wrinkled khakis, worn loafers. She looked past him a moment at the dusty road-worn car, and then back at him. "Is there something you need?"

"Brenda." Sam spoke her name and saw a glimmer of recognition in her eyes.

"Huh?" The voice sounded familiar to her, though a little deeper, and then she saw the mole on his cheek next to his earlobe.

"Sam?"

He nodded.

She was so surprised that she wasn't sure what question she should ask. What are you doing here? What do you want? What brings you back? What do you want from me? All she could manage was an open-ended, "What . . . ?"

Seeing her discomfort, Sam tried to explain as concisely as possible.

"I just wanted to make sure you are okay . . . and I wanted you to know that I'm okay."

Brenda was trembling and she tried to hide it by holding herself as if she was cold, but it was warm and muggy and Sam knew better.

"This might have been a mistake," he offered. "I didn't want to upset you again."

There was a long pause. And then she spoke.

"I didn't know where you were. You just . . . vanished. I didn't want to be married any longer, but that didn't mean I didn't care."

Sam was embarrassed. He wanted to walk away, and without realizing it he took a half step backwards. Brenda reached out for him.

"Wait . . . I'm sorry . . . I didn't mean . . . come in. Please."

Sam followed her through the foyer and into the den. Little had changed, and he found the surroundings uncomfortably familiar. She led him into the kitchen and offered him a glass of iced tea, which he accepted, and then she sat down across from him at the table. And there they sat for an hour and then another hour, gently and calmly sharing their stories of the past two years.

Brenda had advanced at her job, taken a substantial buyout and then bought into a gift shop in Snider Plaza near the university. She had been approached by several men, none of whom Sam knew, but she had chosen not to date and instead concentrated on the business.

"You should have given them a chance," Sam said.

"I was just . . . tired, I suppose. I felt like I didn't have anything else to give. So . . . what about you? I'd heard you left town, but you just disappeared off the radar. Went to chase your fortune somewhere else, I'm sure."

And then Sam shattered that myth by telling her everything there was to tell: How he lived in a trailer near the beach and worked two jobs—at the market and the coffee shop—and had a few friends but otherwise kept to himself. He didn't tell her that just a few days earlier he was piloting a fishing boat through a Gulf storm while an old man lay unconscious on the deck with his daughter tending to him.

"That's some story. Not at all what I would have expected from you," Brenda said.

"Not exactly what I expected either."

"Well I guess it's good to shift gears for a while, get yourself back on track. So . . . what's next for you Sam? Do you have a plan for coming back and starting over?"

Sam looked at his hands wrapped around the tea glass. "I'll go back to Port A in a day or two. Have to get back to work. And I need to return the car I borrowed."

"Port A?"

"That's what we call Port Aransas."

Brenda stared at Sam and realized this was not the man she had known. The aggressive, boastful man she had once been married to had been replaced by a quiet, humble soul. She looked across the table at him and saw in his eyes that he was ready to leave. She hesitated with a question, and then she asked it: "Do you need a place to stay? The guest room hasn't changed."

"No, I have arrangements."

They both stood up from the table, awkwardly but both knowing that the visit was over, and she led him back to the front door.

"Well, then, Sam . . . will I see you again?"

Sam stood in the doorway for a moment, and then answered simply: "We'll see." He smiled for a moment and then turned and walked down the sidewalk. When he looked back toward the door as he got in the car, Brenda had already gone back inside. He drove away knowing he would never be back. Inside, she knew the same thing.

Sam drove away also knowing he had lied to Brenda.

He didn't have a place to stay, but the man that he had become had no problem finding a cheap motel room across the river in an area he would have never entered in his earlier life. And as he lay in bed, staring at the little square television like a cat, he confirmed to himself what Brenda had seen. The man who had once filled board rooms with charisma and bluster, who had been the center of his own universe, who had once loved Brenda or at least liked her enough to marry her, no longer existed.

The next morning Sam crossed the river into Dallas one last time and went back to the tree on the creek and did what he knew he should have done two years earlier: he prayed. He had been questioned and jailed that night and while he'd had some drinks at the party he had never been charged with anything. He had mostly avoided the newspaper reports afterward but he knew that Kayla was from Memphis, and a part of him now wanted to drive to her parents' home, knock on their door, and say something although he had no idea what that might be. Besides, he knew that would be painful for them, so he knelt beside the tree and bowed his head. In silence, he asked God to forgive him, and he asked God to bless Kayla's family and heal their sorrow if that was possible. And when he had emptied his soul, he stood up and dusted the dirt off his knees. It was time to go home.

~ ~ ~ ~ ~

Shelly and Dave were closing down the Dream Bean for the day when Sam rolled up.

"What'd you do with Allie's car?" Dave asked looking out the window at the clean, shiny automobile parked out front.

"Oh, I stopped at the car wash across the bay on the way back. Just wanted to wash off the road grime a little."

"Well it looks like you did more than that," Shelly said. "Allie's gonna like that. Speaking of which, you're just in time."

"For what?"

"Dinner. Allie's cooked dinner and invited us over. We didn't know when you'd be back but I'm sure there's plenty for you, too."

Sam hesitated. "I don't know. I don't want to intrude. I really just wanted to drop off the car."

"Don't be ridiculous. If she knew you were back, she'd insist you come."

To which Dave added: "And if she hears that you are here and you don't come, she'll jump all over us, so you better come. I don't want that girl on my back."

A few minutes later, they all arrived at Allie's bungalow and when Allie opened the door and saw Sam was with Dave and Shelly she threw her arms around him and gave him a big hug, punctuated by a squeal when she looked over his shoulder and saw her car.

"Did you get a good deal for me on the trade-in?" she

joked, which made Sam blush and brought another hug from Allie. "Come on in. You must be tired . . . and starved."

She led the three of them into the little den where Bo was sitting back in a recliner.

"Well look if it ain't the ol' captain himself," Bo said with his usual jest but without his trademark sarcasm. He yanked the lever on the chair, tilted forward with a loud thud, stood up straight and extended his large hand, which Sam accepted.

"You must have flown up there and back," Bo said. "Got all your 'business' done in a hurry, huh?"

"Yes, Sam, what's up with that?" Shelly asked. "You were barely gone forty-eight hours."

"I just . . . took care of things and came back. No reason to stay away longer."

Dave gave Shelly a look that said, "Leave it alone."

"Well, glad you're home."

Allie signaled that it was time to gather around the table, and with everyone standing, she said: "I just want to thank you all for being here with me this evening. And I'm especially pleased that Sam is with us. We'd have had an empty place at the table without him. I think a blessing would be appropriate considering everything that we've all been through recently."

Allie looked around the table at the faces, wanting to pick someone to pray, but she didn't know who to ask. She decided she better do it herself, but then Sam spoke.

"Can I do it?"

"Yes . . . thank you."

Allie reached out and grabbed Bo's hand, and then she nudged him to do the same. Bo reached awkwardly for Shelly's hand, and then Shelly caught Dave's hand—which brought a smile to both of their faces because they had not held hands in public—and then Dave reached for Sam's hand, and Sam took Allie's free hand to complete the chain. Sam cleared his throat, and the others lowered their heads. In that moment of silence, Sam looked at the others—Bo's huge frame leaning forward, Shelly and Dave holding on tight to each other, Allie with her head leaning on her father's shoulder—until he knew what to say.

"Lord . . . we thank you for this day . . . and . . . for these friends especially . . ." Sam stopped a moment and sniffled a little, and then continued, ". . . forgive us when we disappoint each other . . . and most of all . . . when we fail you . . . amen."

With Sam's "amen," chairs clattered and feet shuffled and everyone sat down.

"Hmm," Bo said loudly as they all sat down, "not much of a blessing."

"Huh?" Allie asked, irritated that her father was being his usual ornery self.

"Didn't bless the food at all."

"What do you know about praying?" asked Shelly.

"I prayed once at St. Joseph's."

"Oh yeah? And I bet they prayed you'd never come back." Shelly snorted.

"It was one of those prayer services to send us shrimpers off at the start of the season. I didn't bless the meal either . . . but then there wasn't a meal." He laughed out loud as he picked up his knife and fork.

"Hush and eat. Sam's prayer was just right." Allie knew how heartfelt it had been, because he had let go of her hand for a second, and when he returned his grasp, his fingers were damp.

Chapter 35

One morning the next week while walking to the market, Sam noticed a man carrying boxes from a dusty blue van into the side door of Sea Siren. He didn't give it another thought until a few days later when he was stocking produce and looked up to see Marty with a Sea Siren cup in his hand.

"Hey Marty, how come you never come over to Shelly's? You could get a full breakfast for what you paid for that cup."

"Yeah, I know, but these guys are on my way. I don't do breakfast, anyway, and if I did I sure wouldn't get it over there."

"What are you talking about?" Sam stopped arranging the cucumbers and looked directly at Marty.

"They've got these fancy little bowls full of granola and fruit. And some kind of egg sandwich. Looks okay, but way too expensive."

Marty looked at Sam, who was staring across the store in a kind of trance. "Sam . . . *Sam?*"

The sound of his name brought Sam back. He looked across the store at the clock on the back wall. He wanted to rush out the door but he still had two hours to go on his shift. He also knew he had to be smart about it, so he hashed it out in his head while he stocked shelves. If what Marty said was true, Karl Dexter lied that day in his office when he said he wouldn't compete with Shelly.

When his shift ended, Sam pushed a ten-dollar bill into Marty's hand. "Do me a favor: Tomorrow morning stop by Sea Siren and get yourself a coffee and something to eat . . . and pick up a menu and bring it to me at the Dream Bean."

Marty did as he was told, and when Sam got the menu, he walked out into the alley so he could study it alone. But Shelly saw the exchange between Marty and Sam and she followed him out the back door.

"What's happening, Sam?"

He handed her the piece of paper. She read it, turned it over to look at the back, and then read it again. Her pulse quickened and her face flushed red. "We'll just have to do it better than them."

Sam kicked at the crushed-shell pavement. "You don't understand. They can give it away if they want to. They can outlast us."

"Well . . ." Shelly started to talk, but then she paused, and her shoulders slumped as if all the air had left her body. "You know, Sam, all I wanted to do was have a little place where people could come get a cup of coffee and a muffin on their way to work. Now all of a sudden I'm David facing Goliath."

Sam paced a moment. "Can I have a little time off?"

"Sure. But what are you going to do?"

"I'm going over there."

A few minutes later Sam entered Sea Siren and pushed past the line of customers to the counter. "I need to talk to him."

"Who?" asked the startled young man at the register.

"Karl Dexter."

"He's out till next week."

Sam grabbed an order pad off the counter and pulled the marker out of the young man's apron pocket. He started to write a note and then stopped, tore the page off, and stuffed it in his own pocket. "Never mind," he said, and pushed the marker and pad across the counter.

Sam walked back to the Dream Bean and sat down at a table, winded. Dave had arrived by then and sat down next to him. Nobody was in line so Allie and Shelly joined them.

"Okay, Sam, what'd you find out?" Shelly said.

Sam pulled the page from the order pad out of his pocket and lay it on the table next to the Sea Siren menu. "Look at these. The menu is cheaply printed, no logo, no design standard, doesn't even look like it's the same business as the order pad."

Shelly picked up the menu and looked at it again. "What are you saying?"

"This isn't David and Goliath. This is just Karl. He's gone off the rails."

"Surely they'll catch on and stop him," Dave said.

"I doubt it," Sam said. "Port Aransas is at the end of the world as far as Sea Siren is concerned. They might not come around for six months or a year. As long as the shop is making money on coffee and pastries, they won't question anything."

Dave saw the fear in Shelly's eyes and stood up. "Then I'm going over there myself to put an end to this once and for all."

"He's not there; he's out all week," Sam said.

Dave pulled his phone out of his hip pocket and started to search for a number but Sam reached over and took it out of his hand.

"Who are you calling?" Sam asked.

"Their corporate office . . . the Better Business Bureau . . . state attorney general . . . hell, I don't know . . . but I'm not going to just sit here and let this man ruin what we've built." Dave pulled the phone out of Sam's hand and started fiddling with it again.

"Dave . . . please . . . I'm not talking about doing nothing." Sam began to move for the phone again but Dave backed up a step. His voice rose. "This is Shelly's home, it's her life. It's my life."

"And mine too." Sam was standing now, shouting. "I was here before you in case you've forgotten. I lost everything I had, and now . . . this is *all* that's left for me."

Everyone froze. Customers who had been talking over

cups of coffee were silent. A pair of gulls sitting on the railing outside stopped their bickering. Even the coffee makers hushed their gurgling. The only sound to be heard was the lonely wail of a far-away ship horn. All eyes were on Sam, who was now aware that everyone in the room was looking at him. Embarrassed, he sat down and rested his hands on his knees so that nobody could see his trembling fingers. Then in a hoarse whisper, he said, "Please . . . everyone . . . sit down . . . we have to do this the right way."

The others sat down around the table and waited for Sam to speak again, and when he did it was in slow, measured phrases.

"I know it would make us all feel good to go over there and jump on Karl's back, but we need to be smarter than him. We need to shut him down in a way that will stick. We can't just make a call and turn him in, and there definitely won't be any more talking or handshakes with him." Sam leaned forward and lowered his head. "I know his type . . . too well."

"Okay Sam . . . okay." Shelly sat down beside him. "Let's just all keep our heads and think this through."

The Dream Bean grew silent again except for the hushed conversations of customers, until Marty, who had been quietly eating his Sea Siren breakfast sandwich and listening, spoke from an adjacent table. "You need to scare him."

"Who's that?" Allie whispered.

"He works with me at the market," Sam said. "Go ahead, Marty, what do you have in mind?"

Marty wiped his mouth and walked over to where they were sitting. "The way I see it, you need to catch him cheating—like one of those sting operations on TV—and then jump out and shout, 'Busted!'"

Sam sat up straight. "That's good Marty. That's real good. If we have proof that he's cheating his bosses, he'll have nowhere to turn. He'll have to quit cheating or risk being 'busted' by corporate, as you say."

Everyone was quiet for a moment, and then, one-by-one, the pieces fell into place. Sam suggested that Karl was buying groceries from a wholesaler on his own; that was the van he had seen. Dave reasoned that if Karl was working alone, he was greedy enough to be lured by a cheaper supplier. And then Allie suggested the final piece of the plan: Bo could pose as a bargain wholesaler.

"Bo? That's ridiculous," Shelly said. "He smells like fish from a mile away."

"Not if we polish him up a little," said Sam. "A shave, some decent clothes, a little coaching. Karl told me himself that he spied on us. The rest of us have been seen around here, but nobody at Sea Siren will recognize Bo."

So the plan was set. Marty stopped in at Sea Siren every morning and when he saw that Karl had returned, he alerted Sam. Allie took Bo across the bay to Rockport to buy some khaki slacks and a blue button-down shirt. Bo objected at first, but when he was told that he was going to help "catch a big fish," he was in. "Nobody cheats our Shelly and gets away with it."

Sam and Dave got on Shelly's home computer and created an order sheet with prices well below what Shelly paid at the market. And they gave the company a name: Gulf Discount Produce.

With a blue cap on his head and his makeshift uniform freshly pressed, Bo drove to Sea Siren in a borrowed white van, strode through the front door and asked to speak to the manager.

"What do you need?" Karl asked, stopping to straighten a display as he walked toward Bo.

"I'm here for what you need, and that's some real savings."

Karl looked Bo up and down. "I've already got a supplier."

"But not the best." Bo handed Karl the price sheet.

Karl's eyes worked their way down the sheet, getting bigger with every listing. "Are you kidding me?"

"No sir," and then as rehearsed, Bo made an awkward show of looking at his watch. "Tell you what I'm gonna do: I got deliveries to make so I'll leave this with you and I'll come back tomorrow." He started to walk away but Karl grabbed him by the elbow.

"Hold on there." Karl pulled out a pen and worked his way down the sheet, checking boxes. "I've got what I need for the week, but if you can bring this in on Monday, that'd be great."

"You got it." Bo stuck out his big hand and the two men shook.

Bo climbed into the van and drove down the highway a few blocks and then circled back and parked in the alley behind the Dream Bean. When he walked in the back door, Shelly and the others stopped what they were doing and rushed toward him.

"Well?" Shelly asked.

"Here ya go." Bo pulled the order sheet out of his back pocket and handed it to Sam.

"Great," said Dave. "Now we just have to deliver."

"Monday." Bo took off the cap, tossed it on the counter, and gave his bald head a good rubbing.

"Good enough," said Sam.

Just then Marty came in the front door, excited. "You should have seen him. Bo was completely believable. Karl practically skipped back to his office." As Marty talked, Allie twisted the Sea Siren cup out of his hand and replaced it with a Dream Bean cup.

"Now what was he doing there?" Bo complained. "Didn't trust that I could do it right?"

"We knew you'd do great," Sam said. "I just wanted Marty to watch for things you might not see—like Karl's reaction. Just wanted to see how much he'd swallowed the hook, and it sounds like he took it all."

"Well of course he did. I know how to fish better than any of you."

"Of course you do, Bo." Sam winked at Marty.

So, with the hook set, Dave and Shelly shopped at the market on Sunday evening for everything on Karl's list, being careful to buy cheap generic brands in every category. On Monday morning, Bo pulled up to the side of Sea Siren and delivered the goods. Karl signed the invoice and handed Bo a check.

"Same time next week?" Karl asked.

"Uh . . ." Bo was flustered for a moment; nobody had told him what to say next. But then he looked across the room and saw Marty nodding. "You bet."

A few minutes later, Bo walked into the back of the Dream Bean and handed the check to Sam, who inspected it and then handed it to Shelly. Dave and Allie looked over their shoulders, along with Marty who had raced over from Sea Siren on foot.

"There's our proof," Sam said.

"What?" Shelly asked.

Dave put his hands on Shelly's shoulders. "It's a personal check, honey. You write personal checks for the Dream Bean all the time because it's your business. But Sea Siren should be making purchases on corporate checks."

"Actually, on corporate credit," said Sam.

"He's so busted," Marty crowed.

"Okay . . . so what do we do next? When do we confront him?" Shelly asked.

"Let's go back in there now," Bo said. "Let's yank him into the boat and clean him."

"What do you want to do, Shelly?" Sam asked.

Shelly thought about it for a moment. "Let's wait until Monday. Let his supplies get low and think that more is coming. And then I'd like to be the one to go see him. And I want Sam to go with me."

"I'd be honored," Sam said. "But . . ."

"What?" Shelly asked.

"Oh . . . nothing. I was going to say we need to be civil, but in this case, I think you should just be yourself."

The rest of the week Shelly had a bounce in her step that Dave hadn't seen in a while. She could even be heard humming, and by the weekend her energy was so potent that Dave could not quite contain himself.

"What's gotten into you?" Shelly asked on Saturday night as they cuddled on the sofa while the television flickered across the room. She held his hand tightly to keep it from straying.

"I'm just feeling a little . . . frisky."

"Is that what you call it? I have to admit that I'm liking it." She felt his hand twitch under her clutch. "I'm tempted too, but maybe we should wait. You may not believe it, but underneath this hard-working, she-devil persona I'm a little bit old fashioned and still think a girl should wait."

"Wait? For what?" Dave nuzzled her neck.

"Till she's married, of course."

Dave sighed. "I was afraid you'd say that . . . but . . . I'm glad, too." He rested his head on her shoulder.

"Why is that?" she asked.

"I think it's worth the wait. Like you've said . . . no hurry."

"This is still very nice." She shifted her position and faced him on the sofa. He held her in his arms and they kissed until they were tired and it was time for him to go home.

~ ~ ~ ~ ~

The Dream Bean was closed on Sundays, and without a shift at the market, Sam spent the day on the beach. But instead of just sitting and staring at the breakers as he had done so often, he brought a paperback collection of short stories that someone left on a table at the Dream Bean. He was searching the index for a title that might be interesting when he looked up for a moment and saw a woman walking alone on the edge of the water. Watching her, he became aware of an interest that he hadn't known since he'd been on the island. He'd become so wrapped up in himself that he had let that part of his life wither. To the point that by the time he arrived in Port Aransas, he was numb to any kind of desire. But now, the sight of this woman wearing a long sheer white shirt over the shadow of a red two-piece swimsuit stirred thoughts in him that were fresh, and yet different. While a younger version of him might have marveled at the length and tone of her legs or searched her silhouette for the outline of her breasts, he was more intrigued by the gentle way that her bare feet moved across the sand, and the delicate movement of her fingers as she held her long dark hair behind her ear in the face of the warm afternoon breeze. She seemed to be making a picture in the sand with her foot—perhaps spelling out the name of a secret lover—and as she turned her eyes met Sam's and she smiled and then turned away. She stood back from her drawing and watched as the rising tide erased it, and then she resumed her graceful stroll down the beach.

Sam watched as her form became small and dim in the haze, and then he returned to his book but he had lost his place, so he closed it and rested his chin on his knees. That night, he dreamed of a Spanish dancer on the beach, twirling in a long white skirt, beckoning him to come to her.

Chapter 36

"I need a refill, and I need to see Karl Dexter." Shelly set her Dream Bean cup down hard on the counter, causing the young barista to jump an inch off the floor.

It was Monday morning, a week after Bo delivered the first load of supplies to Sea Siren. But this time it was Shelly and Sam at the counter, and the sight of a Dream Bean cup caused the young man to freeze.

"Better do as she says," Sam said.

Shelly was sipping from the cup when Karl came walking briskly from the back, following the young man and asking, "Where is that van?" But he slowed to a half step and then a full stop when the barista pointed him toward Shelly and Sam.

"Okay you two . . . what do you want?"

"We need to talk." Sam pointed to an empty table near the window. Karl checked his watch, and then shaking his head he followed them to the table. He sat down with his chair as far back from the table as he could without crowding other patrons.

Sam slid one of Karl's menus across the table toward him. Karl craned his neck to see it, and when he recognized it he leaned back in his chair. "So? We have a right to serve breakfast."

Shelly leaned forward. "Yes, technically you do. But you said you wouldn't, and yet you are."

"Well sure . . . I said that, but we have the right to change our mind and do what's good for business."

"Yes, you have that right too," Sam said, "but in this case the 'we' that you're talking about is Karl Dexter and not Sea Siren."

Sam nodded at Shelly, who pulled Karl's check out of her shirt pocket and laid it on the table. Karl's hand moved toward it but Shelly pinned it down with her Dream Bean cup.

Karl scratched his chin. "What, that? I'm just using my own account until corporate sets us up."

"Don't talk to us like we're stupid." Shelly leaned forward even further to close the gap. "Sea Siren is too big for that—and way too big to be buying from a nameless jobber . . . like him."

She pointed to the door, where Bo was standing with a carton of eggs. "Where do you want it?"

"That'll do fine right here," Sam said, touching the middle of the table. Bo walked over, sat down, and set the carton down next to Shelly's cup.

Sam continued: "We checked, and we know that Sea Siren doesn't serve breakfast anywhere. You're doing it on the side. Now, we can do this one of two ways. You can keep your promise and quit serving breakfast, or we can call corporate right now and by tomorrow morning they'll have a new manager here. If my hunch is correct, you've probably been holding back a little profit to make ends meet. You'd probably face charges for that."

"Yeah . . .well . . ." Karl stuttered, and then he started to stand up, but Bo stood up beside him and with his large weathered hand he pressed down on Karl's shoulder until he dropped back into his seat.

Shelly pulled out her cell phone. "Let's see, I put that number in my contacts . . ."

Karl slapped his hand hard on the table, which caused Shelly's coffee cup to tip over and spill toward his lap. Karl skidded his chair backwards to dodge the brown wave and bumped into another table, causing the coffee cups there to wobble until the young man and his girlfriend sitting there grabbed them up.

"What gives, dude?" said the young man angrily.

"Take it easy, you're not hurt," Karl growled, and then he grabbed a handful of napkins to mop up the mess. He looked around, and then he pulled his chair forward and spoke so that only Sam and Shelly could hear. "Okay . . . okay . . . I see where you're going with this. I told corporate they were wasting their time in this sorry swamp of a town, but they wouldn't listen."

"Well you better listen to this, you little . . ." Shelly stopped herself long enough to clean up her mouth but not her attitude. "This sorry swamp, as you call it, is our home and we like it. Our customers live and work here, and they like us. Tourists like us too . . . because we *are* Port Aransas."

Karl glared across the table at her, his arms crossed against his chest.

"I think we're done here." Sam stood up and pulled Shelly's chair back. "Bring the eggs, Bo."

Shelly stood, folded the check, and tucked it into her pocket. "For safekeeping . . . if you know what I mean."

Sam, Shelly, and Bo walked out the front door, but not before Shelly stopped and emptied the rest of her Dream Bean cup into the trash can. She popped the lid back on and carried it out.

Dave and Allie were taking care of business at the Dream Bean when the three of them walked in. Bo carried the eggs to the back and then came out with three in his hand, which he handed to Allie. "Scrambled . . . when you get a chance."

"So . . . how'd it go?" Dave pressed.

Sam looked at Shelly. "What do you think?"

"Well, he acted tough, but I think we scared him . . . and I know we made our point. I don't think he'll cause us any more problems."

And he didn't. Two weeks later, several couples came in to the Dream Bean out of a cool morning rain. "Finally, a hot cup of coffee," one of them said.

"Didn't you see the Sea Siren near the ferry landing?" Allie asked innocently.

"It was closed," one of them said. "Sign on the

window said visit their Corpus Christi location."

"I bet that's the only time that's ever happened—Sea Siren closing a location," said another.

Shelly couldn't believe what she was hearing and shouted to Allie as she bolted out the front door, "Watch the store a minute . . . I've gotta see this for myself."

Shelly sprinted the four blocks, jumped between cars and puddles at the intersection, and didn't stop until she got to the front doors to read the sign taped to the glass. She cupped her hands to look inside and saw that all the tables, chairs, and shelves were gone.

A few minutes later, she dashed back into the front door of the Dream Bean where Dave was waiting with a towel. "Crazy girl," he said, wrapping the towel around her shuddering shoulders. "Last thing we need is for you to get sick. You *are* the Dream Bean, after all."

"No," Shelly said, looking across the room at Bo, Allie, and Sam, "*We* are the Dream Bean."

With the nearest Sea Siren now forty miles around the bay in Corpus Christi, life at the Dream Bean settled down. They never heard what happened to Karl Dexter and why Sea Siren closed, but Sam believed that tourists had been discovering the Dream Bean—because it was near the boats and the docks—and Sea Siren just couldn't sell enough coffee to stay in business.

"I sort of feel sorry about that," Sam said. "They had the right to be in business."

"Yes, but Karl was underhanded about it," Shelly

said. "We couldn't trust him, and neither could his bosses. I'm not gonna lose any sleep worrying about it, and neither should you."

"Still, I didn't really want to hurt anyone . . . especially the local folks they employed."

"Sam . . . there's nothing you should feel sorry about or ashamed of," Dave said. "We were just protecting our interests, and that's serving the people of Port A in a good, honest way."

That was the prevailing opinion as word spread from the docks up the streets and alleyways and into the local shops that the Dream Bean had been victorious in a battle that Sea Siren likely had never lost before. Most of them had never heard of Karl Dexter, so to them it was very much David toppling Goliath.

One morning a group of small business owners, including Maggie from the market, walked into the Dream Bean and crowded around the counter where Shelly was working. One of them spoke:

"Seeing how you all seem to have some experience with this sort of thing, we were thinking the time has come for all of us down here to get organized—in case this type of thing happens again."

"What are you talking about?" Shelly asked.

"We're talking about a group where we all look out for each other and help keep the local businesses strong."

"I think that's a terrific idea," Dave said.

"Well sure, that'd be fine. Count us in," Shelly said.

The man rubbed his jaw a moment. "Well, we were hoping you'd do more than just join. We were hoping you might consider leading the group."

Shelly raised her palms. "Oh no, not me, I could never do something like that. I'm trying to run a business like the rest of you."

Dave agreed. "I think the best person for the job is someone who knows a lot about businesses and how to run them—who can see problems coming, and has a good temperament for working things out."

The group turned their attention to Dave, thinking he was talking about himself, but Dave walked back a few steps and shouted into the kitchen. "Hey, Sam, come out here for a moment."

Sam was washing dishes and had no idea what was going on, and when Dave explained it all, Sam shook his head. "I just can't do that. I've already got two jobs."

Dave faced Sam, but he spoke so that everyone else could hear: "You've done a great job, Sam, but the whole town needs you now. Sea Siren was just the first wave. There are going to be other businesses that don't know a thing about us that are going to want to come in here and take over, and we need someone who can negotiate with them. My guess is," and he glanced at the others as he spoke, "that if we were to ask all the businesses down here to pitch in some annual dues, there'd be enough collected to fund a full-time job."

"Yes, yes," the group said in unison.

Sam shook his head. "I was hoping to free up some time for other things."

"Like what?" Shelly scoffed.

"Maybe he's got a girlfriend he's been hiding," said Bo. "Who knows what goes on down at that trailer?"

"No," said Sam.

"Then what, Sam?" Dave asked.

Sam scratched the top of his head.

"What?" Shelly stomped her foot.

"I want to open a small advertising agency."

"I'll hire you right now," said Maggie. "The only advertising we have is our building. We could use a little help telling people they don't have to go to Corpus or Rockport."

"See, that's perfect," Dave said. "Your clients and association members will be one and the same, but you can branch out to other businesses too. The association and agency can even office together."

"I've got a little building down the street that needs a tenant," said one in the group. "There won't be any rent because I own it."

"And you can move into town. The other side of Dave's duplex is coming available," said Shelly.

"No." Sam looked down at the floor.

"No? What part? The association? The office?"

"The duplex. I'm keeping my trailer. It's my home."

"But . . ." Shelly started to talk but Bo interrupted.

"Let him be. The trailer . . . it's like my boat. It's all

he wants. It's all he needs. Speaking of which, I need to get back on the *Cassie* and start fixing her up."

"Wait a minute now." Allie came around the counter to face her father. "I thought you were finished with that beat-up boat. I thought you said she couldn't be fixed."

"I said she'd be difficult to fix. I never said it couldn't be done, and I never said I wouldn't do it."

Allie pushed Bo into the corner to argue in private while everyone else crowded around Sam to shake hands with the new president of what soon would be dubbed the Port Aransas Pier Association—PAPA.

Chapter 37

Shelly, Allie, and Dave were sitting on the porch of the Dream Bean one late morning when business had slowed down. From the docks they could hear hammering and sawing and general clanging. It was a crew of men that Bo had rounded up to help repair the *Cassie*. Bo said she might not be fit for deep water again, but if she could float, he could still fish the bays. Allie was in the middle of grumbling about how she didn't approve of Bo going back out on the water at all when they heard a loud groan—like wood grinding against wood—a splash and then nothing at all.

"Daddy!" Allie sprang from the porch and ran toward the boat with the others following.

Sam, who was getting settled in to the new office of the Pier Association just a block away, heard the noise and when he looked out the door to see Allie running, he dashed out too. They all reached the pier to find the *Cassie* floating in the water almost up to the top of her pilothouse. Bo was sitting on the roof, and all around him men were thrashing about in the water.

Dave, Shelly, Sam, and Allie spread out around the

boat to help pull the men out of the water. "What happened?" Shelly asked as she gripped a man by the belt and dragged him up onto the pier.

"We were working on her deck and the hull just broke away all of a sudden," said the man as he lay flat on his back. "Never seen anything like it in all my years."

The sight of Bo sitting on the roof of his boat—like a dog on a housetop in a flood—tickled Allie and she couldn't hold back a laugh.

"There's nothing funny about this. What am I supposed to do now?" Bo growled.

"Well the first thing is to get you off the boat," Dave said. Looking around, he found a life preserver on a rope and threw it toward Bo, but the old man just pushed it away and slid off the roof into the water. With a few strong strokes of his arms he pulled himself to a ladder and climbed up with a groan. Bo shook himself off and turned to look at the *Cassie*. The sight of her submerged caused him to lean forward with his hands on his knees. "She's really gone now . . . all that I had."

The other men stood by in silence as if at a graveside. Bo had always been the strongest and toughest of them, pushing back against whatever tide was threatening to drown him. If he ever had doubts or fears, he hid them behind his bark and bluster. But now he was bent over, seemingly defeated.

Allie put her arm around him and helped him straighten up. "She's not *all* that you had." She turned her father away from the *Cassie* and toward the friends that had gathered to help him. "I'd say your nets are pretty full."

"And . . ." Sam started to talk but then paused a moment, hesitant to unveil an idea that had been forming in his head during the days that the *Cassie* had sat lifeless in her berth. It seemed crazy even to him, but then the whole scene was crazy so he pushed his reluctance aside. "The *Cassie's* fishing days may be over, but she's just right for a new purpose."

Allie gave Sam a look that said, "Please don't get Bo's hopes up," but Shelly was curious. "What do you mean?"

"You know that vacant corner of your property, where you've talked about putting a sign that people can see from the highway? I think we can do better."

"What?" Shelly was puzzled until Sam pointed to the submerged boat. "Oh . . . I get it . . . I think."

Allie definitely wasn't getting it, nor was she going to have anything to do with it. She tried to turn Bo away from the scene, but he swung back around. "What are you talking about? What's this got to do with my *Cassie?*" Sam and Dave were huddling with the foreman of the repair crew and didn't hear him.

"You people are crazy." Bo turned and walked off in the direction of Allie's bungalow, throwing off water from his soaked coveralls. Allie followed behind him.

Over the next two weeks Sam's scheme began to

unfold, and as Bo began to hear about it he drew a little closer every day—from Allie's recliner to the porch of the Dream Bean and finally back to the side of the *Cassie*. He didn't fully endorse the plan—"It's as foolish as the men who thought it up," he said—but as long as the name *Cassie* was painted on the stern, he was still the captain. In no time he was barking out orders and grumbling at the "lazy, useless laggards" that were manning the operation.

With the hull of the *Cassie* separated, it didn't take much to pull the deck, gunwale, and pilothouse out of the water intact with a small crane and lifting straps. The hull came up the same way and the pieces were set out to dry for a few days. Meanwhile, on the corner outside the Dream Bean, a bed of sand was laid and a thin concrete slab was poured to the dimensions of the *Cassie's* deck. When everything was ready, the gunwale and bow of the old boat were placed on the perimeter of the slab, and the deck and pilothouse were dropped in on top of that. The effect was a shrimp boat surging up out of the earth toward the street corner.

"She looks great," Bo beamed, admiring how the *Cassie's* prow pointed away from the Dream Bean at an angle that could be seen up and down the street. But then he turned serious. "Now what?"

"That's up to you," Sam said. "But . . . you might want to clean her up, put on a fresh coat of paint and get her ready."

"For what?" Bo was irritated with Sam but also with himself. He'd been so caught up in the work that he hadn't questioned what it was all about. "What the hell are you talking about?"

Shelly filled in the details. "Look, you may not be able to go out on a boat and fish, but you can still fish the piers and the pylons . . . even the beach. And you can bring your catch back to the *Cassie*, put it on ice in the pilothouse, and sell it."

Bo scoffed.

"It's true," Dave said. "Sam and I have been talking around and there'd be a market with the restaurants and the snowbirds too. Like the Dream Bean, you'd only sell whatever you have on hand."

"So . . . Daddy . . . what do you think?" Allie stood on the balls of her feet. She had endorsed the plan wholeheartedly when she understood it would keep her father off the water.

Bo was quiet for a moment, and then he walked up and down the side of the *Cassie* and then onto the deck and into the pilothouse. He came back out into the sunshine. "You'd never know it, but she was a beauty in her day," he said, his voice gone soft for a change. "She was white with blue trim . . . turquoise really. Somebody told me once that when they saw her from a distance she looked like a pearl floating on the water."

Bo came down off the *Cassie* and then turned to look back at her.

"So . . .?" Allie asked again.

"She's gonna need a lot of paint," Bo said.

A collective sigh of relief rose up from the assembly of friends and workers and seemed to stir the palm trees like a gentle gulf breeze.

A couple of weeks later the *Cassie*, boasting a fresh coat of white paint with turquoise trim, was rechristened with a grand celebration that spilled from her decks to the Dream Bean next door. Sam, representing the new PAPA, presented Bo with a rod, reel, and tackle box.

"Now that's not just for show," shouted the owner of one of the restaurants. "We expect you to pull in some fresh catch with that rig."

And then there were calls for a speech, and with prodding from Shelly and Allie, Bo spoke.

"I suppose only a man like Sam over here can understand what it meant to have the *Cassie* as a home. He's got his old trailer, and with a lot of help from all of you, I've still got my *Cassie*. There was a time when that's all I needed. Turns out I need all of you too."

The party continued late into the night—inside the Dream Bean, out on the porch and across the deck of the *Cassie*, where Bo sat in a chair with his feet up on the gunwale just like old times.

Around midnight Sam found Dave and Shelly on the porch, holding hands.

"It's a great night, Sam. Maybe the greatest ever." Shelly said.

Sam couldn't stop a snicker. "Greatest ever?"

"Well, it's the best night in a long time for sure." Shelly held close to Dave but stretched out her free hand for Sam. Shyly, he took it and then turned and leaned against the railing, looking out across the party alongside Shelly and Dave.

"It's definitely a good night," he said.

"It'll be hard to top," Dave said. "So, what's the next big thing, Sam?"

Sam pondered that question for a moment. He'd gotten the **PAPA** office set up and open with a telephone and some supplies. He hadn't started doing any business yet, but the surroundings were comfortable—far different from what he had known in Dallas. The harsh sounds of traffic on the street below and chatter in the offices next door had been replaced by the calming bellows of ship horns and the occasional squawk of a marauding seagull. From his high-rise office in Dallas he looked across the chasm at another nameless tower full of nameless workers. Now he looked past a pair of sea foam-blue drapes to the row of white and pastel shops across the street and beyond them the forest of boat masts and rigging leaning left and right on the water. And just a few doors down, the mast of the *Cassie* stood tall and proud.

"The *Cassie* was just a fortunate opportunity," Sam said, returning to the conversation. "I guess we'll see what tomorrow brings."

"I was talking about you, Sam. What's the next big thing for you?"

Sam didn't have an answer. He was tired and all he could think about was what he wanted to do in the immediate future. "Right now . . . I'm going home and climbing into bed."

"Do you want . . ." Shelly started to say, but Dave squeezed her hand before she finished asking if he wanted a ride. So she just said, "Be careful." She squeezed Sam's hand and then let him go.

"See you in the morning," he said. In a few moments he had turned the corner and was out of sight.

In time, one by one, the other neighbors and guests bid their farewells too and slipped away down the streets to their homes. Allie found her father in his chair on the deck of the *Cassie,* sound asleep. She gently shook him and coaxed him onto his feet and the two walked in the cool night air to their home. That left just Dave and Shelly. When Dave found Shelly picking up cups and napkins and other trash, he took her by the hands and began swaying to the strains of music playing softly.

"That can wait until tomorrow," Dave said. "We'll always have time to clean up, but we won't always have time to dance."

Shelly sank into Dave's arms and swayed with him, her heart beating with the rhythm of the music as she pressed against his chest. She had dreamed of a moment like this but had always thought that it was meant for other girls until this stranger walked into her shop to buy a cup of coffee. And Dave, who thought his dancing days were long over, was back on his feet.

"Hmm . . ." he said softly.

Shelly lifted her head off his shoulder and looked into his eyes. "What was that?"

"Just wondering."

"Wondering?"

"What your answer will be?"

"Answer to what?"

"Answer to the question that I'll ask you some day."

"And what is that question?"

"You'll have to wait."

Shelly put her head back on Dave's shoulder for a moment, but then she raised it up again.

"I don't want to wait. I'll answer now."

"But I haven't asked it yet."

"Yes, you have. You just haven't said it out loud."

"So, then what is your answer?"

"Yes."

"Yes?"

"Yes."

"You sure?"

"Definitely. Now hush . . . and let's dance."

~　~　~　~　~

When Sam reached the trailer park, he paused a moment to listen to the sound of the waves. Drawn by the peaceful rhythm, he walked past the gate and down the blacktop road to the beach like he had so many times and sat down on the warm, dry sand. A full moon spread diamonds of light across the top of the water that rode the breakers and lit up the foam before being deposited on the damp sand in front of him.

As Sam watched the endless, timeless parade of breakers—each one coming in like one day following another—he thought about all the days and nights he had spent in Port Aransas and decided that Shelly was right: This had, in fact, been one of the best nights ever. There was no question that it had been his best night in Port Aransas. It was far different from those first nights of feeling lost and alone, and later, just feeling numb and tired.

And then he thought about what Bo had said—that the *Cassie* had been all he needed, or so he thought until he lost it and needed others to help him get it back, and that Sam understood that need for a place to call home.

Indeed, the trailer had been a place of refuge from the storms that had battered Sam's soul, and a hiding place when the world got too close and threatened to pull him back into the ugliness that he once knew. But he wasn't truly at home until a family of strangers coaxed him out to join them on a journey together. Like Sam, Dave had lost his love, and Bo had seen the work that he knew come to an end. Allie had packed up all she had and moved to another town to find out who she really was.

And Shelly had risked all that she had on a chance to make a life for herself in a little coffee shop on the edge of the world.

Sam smiled. In knowing them, he had forgotten about everything he lost because they each had given him something that was missing—a small, simple taste of the grace of God. That was all he had ever really needed.

About the Author

Jeff Hampton has based his life and career in Texas writing for newspapers, magazines, businesses, and institutions. His interest in observing the people around him has led him to write essays, short stories, and novels that explore relationships and communities in their many forms.

Aransas Morning is his fifth book, following *Grandpa Jack*, *When the Light Returned to Main Street*, *Jonah Prophet*, and *The Snowman Uprising on Hickory Lane*.

Watch for *Aransas Evening*, a sequel to *Aransas Morning*, in 2018.

www.jeffhamptonwriter.com